Dorothy and the Wizard in Oz

L. Frank Baum

A WATERMILL CLASSIC

Chapter 1
The Earthquake

The train from 'Frisco was very late. It should have arrived at Hugson's Siding at midnight, but it was already five o'clock and the gray dawn was breaking in the east when the little train slowly rumbled up to the open shed that served for the station house. As it came to a stop the conductor called out in a loud voice:

"Hugson's Siding!"

At once a little girl rose from her seat and walked to the door of the car, carrying a wicker suitcase in one hand and a round birdcage covered with newspapers in the other, while a parasol was tucked under her arm. The conductor helped her off the car and then the engineer started his train again, so that it puffed and groaned and moved slowly away up the track. The reason he was so late was because all through the night there were times when the solid earth shook and trembled under him, and the engineer was afraid that at any moment the rails might spread apart and an accident happen to his passengers. So he moved the cars slowly and with caution.

The little girl stood still to watch until the train had disappeared around a curve; then she turned to see where she was.

The shed at Hugson's Siding was bare save for an old wooden bench, and did not look very inviting. As she peered through the soft gray light not a house of any sort was visible near the station, nor was any person in sight; but after a while the child discovered a horse and buggy standing near a group of trees a short distance away. She walked toward it and found the horse tied to a tree and standing motionless, with its head hanging down almost to the ground. It was a big horse, tall and bony, with long legs and large knees and feet. She could count his ribs easily where they showed through the skin of his body, and his head was long and seemed altogether too big for him, as if it did not fit. His tail was short and scraggly, and his harness had been broken in many places and fastened together again with cords and bits of wire. The buggy seemed almost new, for it had a shiny top and side curtains. Getting around in front so that she could look inside, the girl saw a boy curled up on the seat, fast asleep.

She set down the birdcage and poked the boy with her parasol. Presently he woke up, rose to a sitting position and rubbed his eyes briskly.

"Hello!" he said, seeing her. "Are you Dorothy Gale?"

"Yes," she answered, looking gravely at his tousled hair and blinking gray eyes. "Have you come to take me to Hugson's Ranch?"

"Of course," he answered. "Train in?"

"I couldn't be here if it wasn't," she said.

He laughed at that, and his laugh was merry and frank. Jumping out of the buggy he put Dorothy's suitcase under the seat and her bird-cage on the floor in front.

"Canary birds?" he asked.

"Oh, no; it's just Eureka, my kitten. I thought that was the best way to carry her."

The boy nodded.

"Eureka's a funny name for a cat," he remarked.

"I named my kitten that because I found it," she explained. "Uncle Henry says 'Eureka' means 'I have found it.'"

"All right; hop in."

She climbed into the buggy and he followed her. Then the boy picked up the reins, shook them, and said "Gid-dap!"

The horse did not stir. Dorothy thought he just wiggled one of his drooping ears, but that was all.

"Gid-dap!" called the boy, again.

The horse stood still.

"Perhaps," said Dorothy, "if you untied him, he would go."

The boy laughed cheerfully and jumped out.

"Guess I'm half asleep yet," he said, untying the horse. "But Jim knows his business all right —don't you, Jim?" patting the long nose of the animal.

Then he got into the buggy again and took the reins, and the horse at once backed away from the tree, turned slowly around, and began to trot down the sandy road which was just visible in the dim light.

"Thought that train would never come," observed the boy. "I've waited at that station for five hours."

"We had a lot of earthquakes," said Dorothy. "Didn't you feel the ground shake?"

"Yes; but we're used to such things in California," he replied. "They don't scare us much."

"The conductor said it was the worst quake he ever knew."

"Did he? Then it must have happened while I was asleep," he said thoughtfully.

"How is Uncle Henry?" she inquired, after a pause during which the horse continued to trot with long, regular strides.

"He's pretty well. He and Uncle Hugson have been having a fine visit."

"Is Mr. Hugson your uncle?" she asked.

"Yes. Uncle Bill Hugson married your Uncle Henry's wife's sister; so we must be second cousins," said the boy in an amused tone. "I work for Uncle Bill on his ranch, and he pays me six dollars a month and my board."

"Isn't that a great deal?" she asked, doubtfully.

"Why, it's a great deal for Uncle Hugson, but not for me. I'm a splendid worker. I work as well as I sleep," he added with a laugh.

"What is your name?" asked Dorothy, thinking she liked the boy's manner and the cheery tone of his voice.

4

"Not a very pretty one," he answered, as if a little ashamed. "My whole name is Zebediah; but folks just call me 'Zeb.' You've been to Australia, haven't you?"

"Yes; with Uncle Henry," she answered. "We got to San Francisco a week ago, and Uncle Henry went right on to Hugson's Ranch for a visit while I stayed a few days in the city with some friends we had met."

"How long will you be with us?" he asked.

"Only a day. Tomorrow Uncle Henry and I must start back for Kansas. We've been away for a long time, you know, and so we're anxious to get home again."

The boy flicked the big, bony horse with his whip and looked thoughtful. Then he started to say something to his little companion, but before he could speak the buggy began to sway dangerously from side to side and the earth seemed to rise up before them. Next minute there was a roar and a sharp crash, and at her side Dorothy saw the ground open in a wide crack and then come together again.

"Goodness!" she cried, grasping the iron rail of the seat. "What was that?"

"That was an awful big quake," replied Zeb, with a white face. "It almost got us that time, Dorothy."

The horse had stopped short, and stood firm as a rock. Zeb shook the reins and urged him to go, but Jim was stubborn. Then the boy cracked his whip and touched the animal's flanks with it, and after a low moan of protest Jim stepped slowly along the road.

Neither the boy nor the girl spoke again for some minutes. There was a breath of danger in the very air, and every few moments the earth would shake violently. Jim's ears were standing erect upon his head and every muscle of his big body was tense as he trotted toward home. He was not going very fast, but on his flanks specks of foam began to appear and at times he would tremble like a leaf.

The sky had grown darker again and the wind made queer sobbing sounds as it swept over the valley.

Suddenly there was a rending, tearing sound, and the earth split into another great crack just beneath the spot where the horse was standing. With a wild neigh of terror the animal fell bodily into the pit, drawing the buggy and its occupants after him.

Dorothy grabbed fast hold of the buggy top and the boy did the same. The sudden rush into space confused them so that they could not think.

Blackness engulfed them on every side, and in breathless silence they waited for the fall to end and crush them against jagged rocks or for the earth to close in on them again and bury them forever in its dreadful depths.

The horrible sensation of falling, the darkness and the terrifying noises, proved more than Dorothy could endure and for a few moments the little girl lost consciousness. Zeb, being a boy, did not faint, but he was badly frightened, and clung to the buggy seat with a tight grip, expecting every moment would be his last.

Chapter 2
The Glass City

When Dorothy recovered her senses they were still falling, but not so fast. The top of the buggy caught the air like a parachute or an umbrella filled with wind, and held them back so that they floated downward with a gentle motion that was not so very disagreeable to bear. The worst thing was their terror of reaching the bottom of this great crack in the earth, and the natural fear that sudden death was about to overtake them at any moment. Crash after crash echoed far above their heads, as the earth came together where it had split, and stones and chunks of clay rattled around them on every side. These they could not see, but they could feel them pelting the buggy top, and Jim screamed almost like a human being when a stone overtook him and struck his bony body. They did not really hurt the poor horse, because everything was falling together; only the stones and rubbish fell faster than the horse and buggy, which were held back by the pressure of the air, so that the terrified animal was actually more frightened than he was injured.

How long this state of things continued Dorothy could not even guess, she was so greatly bewildered. But by and by, as she stared ahead into the black chasm with a beating heart, she began to dimly see the form of the horse Jim —his head up in the air, his ears erect and his long legs sprawling in every direction as he tumbled through space. Also, turning her head, she found that she could see the boy beside her, who had until now remained as still and silent as she herself.

Dorothy sighed and commenced to breathe easier. She began to realize that death was not in store for her, after all, but that she had merely started upon another adventure, which promised to be just as queer and unusual as were those she had before encountered.

With this thought in mind the girl took heart and leaned her head over the side of the buggy to see where the strange light was coming from. Far below her she found six great glowing balls suspended in the air. The central and largest one was white, and reminded her of the sun. Around it were arranged, like the five points of a star, the other five brilliant balls; one being rose-colored, one violet, one yellow, one blue and one orange. This splendid group of colored suns sent rays darting in every direction, and as the horse and buggy—with Dorothy and Zeb—sank steadily downward and came nearer to the lights, the rays began to take on all the delicate tintings of a rainbow, growing more and more distinct every moment until all the space was brilliantly illuminated.

Dorothy was too dazed to say much, but she watched one of Jim's big ears turn to violet and the other to rose, and wondered that his tail should be yellow and his body striped with blue and orange like the stripes of a zebra. Then she looked at Zeb, whose face was blue and whose hair was pink, and gave a little laugh that sounded a bit nervous.

"Isn't it funny?" she said.

The boy was startled and his eyes were big. Dorothy had a green streak through the center of her face where the blue and yellow lights came together, and her appearance seemed to add to his fright.

"I—I don't s-s-see any-thing funny—'bout it!" he stammered.

Just then the buggy tipped slowly over upon its side, the body of the horse tipping also. But they continued to fall, all together, and the boy and girl had no difficulty in remaining upon the seat, just as they were before. Then they turned bottom side up, and continued to roll slowly over until they were right side up again. During this time Jim struggled frantically, all his legs kicking the air; but on finding himself in his former position the horse said, in a relieved tone of voice:

"Well, that's better!"

Dorothy and Zeb looked at one another in wonder.

"Can your horse talk?" she asked.

"Never knew him to before," replied the boy.

"Those were the first words I ever said," called out the horse, who had overheard them, "and I can't explain why I happened to speak then. This is a nice scrape you've got me into, isn't it?"

"As for that, we are in the same scrape ourselves," answered Dorothy cheerfully. "But never mind; something will happen pretty soon."

"Of course," growled the horse, "and then we shall be sorry it happened."

Zeb gave a shiver. All this was so terrible and unreal that he could not understand it at all, and so had good reason to be afraid.

Swiftly they drew near to the flaming colored suns, and passed close beside them. The light was then so bright that it dazzled their eyes, and they covered their faces with their hands to escape being blinded. There was no heat in the colored suns, however, and after they had passed below them the top of the buggy shut out many of the piercing rays so that the boy and girl could open their eyes again.

"We've got to come to the bottom some time," remarked Zeb, with a deep sigh. "We can't keep falling forever, you know."

"Of course not," said Dorothy. "We are somewhere in the middle of the earth, and the chances are we'll reach the other side of it before long. But it's a big hollow, isn't it?"

"Awful big!" answered the boy.

"We're coming to something now," announced the horse.

At this they both put their heads over the side

of the buggy and looked down. Yes; there was land below them; and not so very far away, either. But they were floating very, very slowly —so slowly that it could no longer be called a fall—and the children had ample time to take heart and look about them.

They saw a landscape with mountains and plains, lakes and rivers, very like those upon the earth's surface; but all the scene was splendidly colored by the variegated lights from the six suns. Here and there were groups of houses that seemed made of clear glass, because they sparkled so brightly.

"I'm sure we are in no danger," said Dorothy, in a sober voice. "We are falling so slowly that we can't be dashed to pieces when we land, and this country that we are coming to seems quite pretty."

"We'll never get home again though!" declared Zeb, with a groan.

"Oh, I'm not so sure of that," replied the girl. "But don't let us worry over such things, Zeb; we can't help ourselves just now, you know, and I've always been told it's foolish to borrow trouble."

The boy became silent, having no reply to so sensible a speech, and soon both were fully occupied in staring at the strange scenes spread out below them. They seemed to be falling right into the middle of a big city which had many tall buildings with glass domes and sharp-pointed spires. These spires were like great spear points, and if they tumbled upon one of them they were likely to suffer serious injury.

Jim the horse had seen these spires, also, and his ears stood straight up with fear, while Dorothy and Zeb held their breaths in suspense. But no; they floated gently down upon a broad, flat roof, and came to a stop at last.

When Jim felt something firm under his feet the poor beast's legs trembled so much that he could hardly stand; but Zeb at once leaped out of the buggy to the roof, and he was so awkward and hasty that he kicked over Dorothy's bird-cage, which rolled out upon the roof so that the bottom came off. At once a pink kitten crept out of the upset cage, sat down upon the glass roof, and yawned and blinked its round eyes.

"Oh," said Dorothy. "There's Eureka."

"First time I ever saw a pink cat," said Zeb.

"Eureka isn't pink; she's white. It's this queer light that gives her that color."

"Where's my milk?" asked the kitten, looking up into Dorothy's face. "I'm 'most starved to death."

"Oh, Eureka! Can you talk?"

"Talk! Am I talking? Good gracious, I believe I am. Isn't it funny?" asked the kitten.

"It's all wrong," said Zeb gravely. "Animals ought not to talk. But even old Jim has been saying things since we had our accident."

"I can't see that it's wrong," remarked Jim in his gruff tones. "At least, it isn't as wrong as some other things. What's going to become of us now?"

"I don't know," answered the boy, looking around him curiously.

The houses of the city were all made of glass, so clear and transparent that one could look through the walls as easily as through a window. Dorothy saw, underneath the roof on which she stood, several rooms used for rest chambers, and even thought she could make out a number of queer forms huddled into the corners of these rooms.

The roof beside them had a great hole smashed through it, and pieces of glass were lying scattered in every direction. A nearby steeple had been broken off short and the fragments lay heaped beside it. Other buildings were cracked in places or had corners chipped off from them; but they must have been very beautiful before these accidents had happened to mar their perfection. The rainbow tints from the colored suns fell upon the glass city softly and gave to the buildings many delicate, shifting hues which were very pretty to see.

But not a sound had broken the stillness since the strangers had arrived, except that of their own voices. They began to wonder if there were no people to inhabit this magnificent city of the inner world.

Suddenly a man appeared through a hole in the roof next to the one they were on and stepped into plain view. He was not a very large man, but was well-formed and had a beautiful face— calm and serene as the face of a fine portrait. His clothing fitted his form snugly and was gorgeously colored in brilliant shades of green, which varied as the sunbeams touched them but was not wholly influenced by the solar rays.

The man had taken a step or two across the glass roof before he noticed the presence of the strangers; but then he stopped abruptly. There was no expression of either fear or surprise upon his tranquil face, yet he must have been both astonished and afraid; for after his eyes had rested upon the ungainly form of the horse for a moment he walked rapidly to the furthest edge of the roof, his head turned back over his shoulder to gaze at the strange animal.

"Look out!" cried Dorothy, who noticed that the beautiful man did not look where he was going; "be careful, or you'll fall off!"

But he paid no attention to her warning. He reached the edge of the tall roof, stepped one foot out into the air, and walked into space as calmly as if he were on firm ground.

The girl, greatly astonished, ran to lean over the edge of the roof, and saw the man walking rapidly through the air toward the ground. Soon he reached the street and disappeared through a glass doorway into one of the glass buildings.

"How strange!" she exclaimed, drawing a long breath.

"Yes; but it's lots of fun, if it *is* strange," remarked the small voice of the kitten, and Dorothy turned to find her pet walking in the air a foot or so away from the edge of the roof.

"Come back, Eureka!" she called, in distress, "you'll certainly be killed."

"I have nine lives," said the kitten, purring softly as it walked around in a circle and then came back to the roof, "but I can't lose even one of them by falling in this country, because I really couldn't manage to fall if I wanted to.''

"Does the air bear up your weight?'' asked the girl.

"Of course; can't you see?'' and again the kitten wandered into the air and back to the edge of the roof.

"It's wonderful!'' said Dorothy.

"Suppose we let Eureka go down to the street and get someone to help us,'' suggested Zeb, who had been even more amazed than Dorothy at these strange happenings.

"Perhaps we can walk on the air ourselves,'' replied the girl.

Zeb drew back with a shiver.

"I wouldn't dare try,'' he said.

"Maybe Jim will go,'' continued Dorothy, looking at the horse.

"And maybe he won't!'' answered Jim. "I've tumbled through the air long enough to make me contented on this roof.''

"But we didn't tumble to the roof,'' said the girl. "By the time we reached here we were floating very slowly, and I'm almost sure we could float down to the street without getting hurt. Eureka walks on the air all right.''

"Eureka weighs only about half a pound,'' replied the horse in a scornful tone, "while I weigh about half a ton.''

"You don't weigh as much as you ought to, Jim,'' remarked the girl, shaking her head as she looked at the animal. "You're dreadfully skinny.''

"Oh, well; I'm old," said the horse, hanging his head despondently, "and I've had lots of trouble in my day, little one. For a good many years I drew a public cab in Chicago, and that's enough to make anyone skinny."

"He eats enough to get fat, I'm sure," said the boy gravely.

"Do I? Can you remember any breakfast that I've had today?" growled Jim, as if he resented Zeb's speech.

"None of us has had breakfast," said the boy, "and in a time of danger like this it's foolish to talk about eating."

"Nothing is more dangerous than being without food," declared the horse, with a sniff at the rebuke of his young master, "and just at present no one can tell whether there are any oats in this queer country or not. If there are, they are liable to be glass oats!"

"Oh, no!" exclaimed Dorothy. "I can see plenty of nice gardens and fields down below us, at the edge of this city. But I wish we could find a way to get to the ground."

"Why don't you walk down?" asked Eureka. "I'm as hungry as the horse is, and I want my milk."

"Will you try it, Zeb?" asked the girl, turning to her companion.

Zeb hesitated. He was still pale and frightened, for this dreadful adventure had upset him and made him nervous and worried. But he did not wish the little girl to think him a coward, so he advanced slowly to the edge of the roof.

Dorothy stretched out a hand to him and Zeb put one foot out and let it rest in the air a little over the edge of the roof. It seemed firm enough to walk upon, so he took courage and put out the other foot. Dorothy kept hold of his hand and followed him, and soon they were both walking through the air, with the kitten frisking beside them.

"Come on, Jim!" called the boy. "It's all right."

Jim had crept to the edge of the roof to look over, and being a sensible horse and quite experienced, he made up his mind that he could go where the others did. So, with a snort and a neigh and a whisk of his short tail, he trotted off the roof into the air and at once began floating downward to the street. His great weight made him fall faster than the children walked, and he passed them on the way down; but when he came to the glass pavement he alighted upon it so softly that he was not even jarred.

"Well, well!" said Dorothy, drawing a long breath. "What a strange country this is."

People began to come out of the glass doors to look at the new arrivals, and pretty soon quite a crowd had assembled. There were men and women, but no children at all, and the folks were all beautifully formed and attractively dressed and had wonderfully handsome faces. There was not an ugly person in all the throng, yet Dorothy was not especially pleased by the appearance of these people because their features had no more expression than the faces of dolls. They did not smile nor did they frown, or show either fear or surprise or curiosity or friendliness. They simply stared at the strangers, paying most attention to Jim and Eureka, for they had never before seen either a horse or a cat and the children bore an outward resemblance to themselves.

Pretty soon a man joined the group who wore a glistening star in the dark hair just over his forehead. He seemed to be a person of authority, for the others pressed back to give him room. After turning his composed eyes first upon the animals and then upon the children, he said to Zeb, who was a little taller than Dorothy:

"Tell me, intruder, was it you who caused the Rain of Stones?"

For a moment the boy did not know what he meant by this question. Then, remembering the stones that had fallen with them and passed them long before they had reached this place, he answered:

"No, sir; we didn't cause anything. It was the earthquake."

The man with the star stood for a time quietly thinking over this speech. Then he asked:

"What is an earthquake?"

"I don't know," said Zeb, who was still confused. But Dorothy, seeing his perplexity, answered:

"It's a shaking of the earth. In this quake a big crack opened and we fell through—horse and buggy, and all—and the stones got loose and came down with us."

The man with the star regarded her with his calm, expressionless eyes.

"The Rain of Stones has done much damage to our city," he said; "and we shall hold you responsible for it unless you can prove your innocence."

"How can we do that?" asked the girl.

"That I am not prepared to say. It is your affair, not mine. You must go to the House of the Sorcerer, who will soon discover the truth."

"Where is the House of the Sorcerer?" the girl inquired.

"I will lead you to it. Come!"

He turned and walked down the street, and after a moment's hesitation Dorothy caught Eureka in her arms and climbed into the buggy. The boy took his seat beside her and said: "Giddap, Jim."

As the horse ambled along, drawing the buggy, the people of the glass city made way for them and formed a procession in their rear. Slowly they moved down one street and up another, turning first this way and then that, until they came to an open square in the center of which was a big glass palace having a central dome and four tall spires on each corner.

Chapter 3
The Arrival of the Wizard

The doorway of the glass palace was quite big enough for the horse and buggy to enter, so Zeb drove straight through it and the children found themselves in a lofty hall that was very beautiful. The people at once followed and formed a circle around the sides of the spacious room, leaving the horse and buggy and the man with the star to occupy the center of the hall.

"Come to us, oh, Gwig!" called the man, in a loud voice.

Instantly a cloud of smoke appeared and rolled over the floor; then it slowly spread and ascended into the dome, disclosing a strange personage seated upon a glass throne just before Jim's nose. He was formed just as were the other inhabitants of this land and his clothing only differed from theirs in being bright yellow. But he had no hair at all, and all over his bald head and face and upon the backs of his hands grew sharp thorns like those found on the branches of rosebushes. There was even a thorn upon the tip of his nose and he looked so funny that Dorothy laughed when she saw him.

The Sorcerer, hearing the laugh, looked toward the little girl with cold, cruel eyes, and his glance made her grow sober in an instant.

"Why have you dared to intrude your unwelcome persons into the secluded Land of the Mangaboos?" he asked sternly.

"'Cause we couldn't help it," said Dorothy.

"Why did you wickedly and viciously send the Rain of Stones to crack and break our houses?" he continued.

"We didn't," declared the girl.

"Prove it!" cried the Sorcerer.

"We don't have to prove it," answered Dorothy, indignantly. "If you had any sense at all, you'd have known it was the earthquake."

"We only know that yesterday came a Rain of Stones upon us, which did much damage and injured some of our people. Today came another Rain of Stones, and soon after it you appeared among us."

"By the way," said the man with the star, looking steadily at the Sorcerer, "you told us yesterday that there would not be a second Rain of Stones. Yet one has just occurred that was even worse than the first. What is your sorcery good for if it cannot tell us the truth?"

"My sorcery does tell the truth!" declared the thorn-covered man. "I said there would be but one Rain of Stones. This second one was a Rain of People-and-Horse-and-Buggy. And some stones came with them."

"Will there by any more Rains?" asked the man with the star.

"No, my Prince."

"Neither stones nor people?"

"No, my Prince."

"Are you sure?"

"Quite sure, my Prince. My sorcery tells me so."

Just then a man came running into the hall and addressed the Prince after making a low bow.

"More wonders in the air, my Lord," said he.

Immediately the Prince and all his people flocked out of the hall into the street, that they might see what was about to happen. Dorothy and Zeb jumped out of the buggy and ran after them, but the Sorcerer remained calmly in his throne.

Far up in the air was an object that looked like a balloon. It was not so high as the glowing star of the six colored suns, but was descending slowly through the air—so slowly that at first it scarcely seemed to move.

The throng stood still and waited. It was all they could do, for to go away and leave that strange sight was impossible; nor could they hurry its fall in any way. The earth children were not noticed, being so near the average size of the Mangaboos, and the horse had remained in the House of the Sorcerer, with Eureka curled up asleep on the seat of the buggy.

Gradually the balloon grew bigger, which was proof that it was settling down upon the Land of the Mangaboos. Dorothy was surprised to find how patient the people were, for her own little heart was beating rapidly with excitement. A balloon meant to her some other arrival from the surface of the earth, and she hoped it would be someone able to assist her and Zeb out of their difficulties.

In an hour the balloon had come near enough for her to see a basket suspended below it; in two hours she could see a head looking over the side of the basket; in three hours the big balloon settled slowly into the great square in which they stood and came to rest on the glass pavement.

Then a little man jumped out of the basket, took off his tall hat, and bowed very gracefully to the crowd of Mangaboos around him. He was quite an old little man, and his head was long and entirely bald.

"Why," cried Dorothy, in amazement, "it's Oz!"

The little man looked toward her and seemed as much surprised as she was. But he smiled and bowed as he answered:

"Yes, my dear; I am Oz, the Great and Terrible. Eh? And you are little Dorothy, from Kansas. I remember you very well."

"Who did you say it was?" whispered Zeb to the girl.

"It's the wonderful Wizard of Oz. Haven't you heard of him?"

Just then the man with the star came and stood before the Wizard.

"Sir," said he, "why are you here, in the Land of the Mangaboos?"

"Didn't know what land it was, my son," returned the other, with a pleasant smile; "and, to be honest, I didn't mean to visit you when I started out. I live on top of the earth, your honor, which is far better than living inside it; but yesterday I went up in a balloon, and when I came down I fell into a big crack in the earth, caused by an earthquake. I had let so much gas out of my balloon that I could not rise again, and in a few minutes the earth closed over my head. So I continued to descend until I reached this place, and if you will show me a way to get out of it, I'll go with pleasure. Sorry to have troubled you, but it couldn't be helped.''

The Prince had listened with attention. Said he:

''This child, who is from the crust of the earth, like yourself, called you a Wizard. Is not a Wizard something like a Sorcerer?''

''It's better,'' replied Oz promptly. ''One Wizard is worth three Sorcerers.''

''Ah, you shall prove that,'' said the Prince. ''We Mangaboos have, at the present time, one of the most wonderful Sorcerers that ever was picked from a bush; but he sometimes makes mistakes. Do you ever make mistakes?''

''Never!'' declared the Wizard boldly.

''Oh, Oz!'' said Dorothy. ''You made a lot of mistakes when you were in the marvelous Land of Oz.''

''Nonsense!'' said the little man, turning red—although just then a ray of violet sunlight was on his round face.

''Come with me,'' said the Prince to him. ''I wish you to meet our Sorcerer.''

The Wizard did not like this invitation, but he

could not refuse to accept it. So he followed the Prince into the great domed hall, and Dorothy and Zeb came after them, while the throng of people trooped in also.

There sat the thorny Sorcerer in his chair of state, and when the Wizard saw him he began to laugh, uttering comical little chuckles.

"What an absurd creature!" he exclaimed.

"He may look absurd," said the Prince in his quiet voice, "but he is an excellent Sorcerer. The only fault I find with him is that he is so often wrong."

"I am never wrong," answered the Sorcerer.

"Only a short time ago you told me there would be no more Rain of Stones or of People," said the Prince.

"Well, what then?"

"Here is another person descended from the air to prove you were wrong."

"One person cannot be called 'people,'" said the Sorcerer. "If two should come out of the sky you might with justice say I was wrong; but unless more than this one appears I will hold that I was right."

"Very clever," said the Wizard, nodding his head as if pleased. "I am delighted to find humbugs inside the earth, just the same as on top of it. Were you ever with a circus, brother?"

"No," said the Sorcerer.

"You ought to join one," declared the little man seriously. "I belong to Bailum & Barney's Great Consolidated Shows—three rings in one tent and a menagerie on the side. It's a fine aggregation, I assure you."

"What do you do?" asked the Sorcerer.

"I go up in a balloon, usually, to draw the crowds to the circus. But I've just had the bad luck to come out of the sky, skip the solid earth, and land lower down than I intended. But never mind. It isn't everybody who gets a chance to see your Land of the Gabazoos."

"Mangaboos," said the Sorcerer, correcting him. "If you are a Wizard you ought to be able to call people by their right names."

"Oh, I'm a Wizard; you may be sure of that. Just as good a Wizard as you are a Sorcerer."

"That remains to be seen," said the other.

"If you are able to prove that you are better," said the Prince to the little man, "I will make you the Chief Wizard of this domain. Otherwise—"

"What will happen otherwise?" asked the Wizard.

"I will stop you from living, and forbid you to be planted," returned the Prince.

"That does not sound especially pleasant," said the little man, looking at the one with the star uneasily. "But never mind. I'll beat Old Prickly, all right."

"My name is Gwig," said the Sorcerer, turning his heartless, cruel eyes upon his rival. "Let me see you equal the sorcery I am about to perform."

He waved a thorny hand and at once the tinkling of bells was heard, playing sweet music. Yet, look where she would, Dorothy could discover no bells at all in the great glass hall.

The Mangaboo people listened, but showed no great interest. It was one of the things Gwig usually did to prove he was a sorcerer.

Now was the Wizard's turn, so he smiled upon the assemblage and asked:

"Will somebody kindly loan me a hat?"

No one did, because the Mangaboos did not wear hats, and Zeb had lost his, somehow, in his flight through the air.

"Ahem!" said the Wizard. "Will somebody please loan me a handkerchief?"

But they had no handkerchiefs either.

"Very good," remarked the Wizard. "I'll use my own hat, if you please. Now, good people, observe me carefully. You see, there is nothing up my sleeve and nothing concealed about my person. Also, my hat is quite empty." He took off his hat and held it upside down, shaking it briskly.

"Let me see it," said the Sorcerer.

He took the hat and examined it carefully, returning it afterward to the Wizard.

"Now," said the little man, "I will create something out of nothing."

He placed the hat upon the glass floor, made a pass with his hand, and then removed the hat, displaying a little white piglet no bigger than a mouse, which began to run around here and there and to grunt and squeal in a tiny, shrill voice.

The people watched it intently, for they had never seen a pig before, big or little. The Wizard reached out, caught the wee creature in his hand, and holding its head between one thumb and finger and its tail between the other thumb and finger he pulled it apart, each of the two parts becoming a whole and separate piglet in an instant.

He placed one upon the floor, so that it could run around, and pulled apart the other, making three piglets in all; and then one of these was pulled apart, making four piglets. The Wizard continued this surprising performance until nine tiny piglets were running about at his feet, all squealing and grunting in a very comical way.

"Now," said the Wizard of Oz, "having created something from nothing, I will make something nothing again."

With this he caught up two of the piglets and pushed them together, so that the two were one. Then he caught up another piglet and pushed it into the first, where it disappeared. And so, one by one, the nine tiny piglets were pushed together until but a single one of the creatures remained. This the Wizard placed underneath his hat and made a mystic sign above it. When he removed his hat the last piglet had disappeared entirely.

The little man gave a bow to the silent throng that had watched him, and then the Prince said, in his cold, calm voice:

"You are indeed a wonderful Wizard, and your powers are greater than those of my Sorcerer."

"He will not be a wonderful Wizard long," remarked Gwig.

"Why not?" inquired the Wizard.

"Because I am going to stop your breath," was the reply. "I perceive that you are curiously constructed, and that if you cannot breathe you cannot keep alive."

The little man looked troubled.

"How long will it take you to stop my breath?" he asked.

"About five minutes. I'm going to begin now. Watch me carefully."

He began making queer signs and passes toward the Wizard; but the little man did not watch him long. Instead, he drew a leather case from his pocket and took from it several sharp knives, which he joined together, one after another, until they made a long sword. By the time he had attached a handle to this sword he was having much trouble to breathe, as the charm of the Sorcerer was beginning to take effect.

So the Wizard lost no more time, but leaping forward he raised the sharp sword, whirled it once or twice around his head, and then gave a mighty stroke that cut the body of the Sorcerer exactly in two.

Dorothy screamed and expected to see a terrible sight; but as the two halves of the Sorcerer fell apart on the floor she saw that he had no bones or blood inside of him at all, and that the place where he was cut looked much like a sliced turnip or potato.

"Why, he's vegetable!" cried the Wizard, astonished.

"Of course," said the Prince. "We are all vegetable, in this country. Are you not vegetable also?"

"No," answered the Wizard. "People on top of the earth are all meat. Will your Sorcerer die?"

"Certainly, sir. He is really dead now, and

will wither very quickly. So we must plant him at once, that other Sorcerers may grow upon his bush,'' continued the Prince.

''What do you mean by that?'' asked the little Wizard, greatly puzzled.

''If you will accompany me to our public gardens,'' replied the Prince, ''I will explain to you much better than I can here the mysteries of our Vegetable Kingdom.''

Chapter 4

The Vegetable Kingdom

After the Wizard had wiped the dampness from his sword and taken it apart and put the pieces into their leather case again, the man with the star ordered some of his people to carry the two halves of the Sorcerer to the public gardens.

Jim pricked up his ears when he heard they were going to the gardens, and wanted to join the party, thinking he might find something proper to eat; so Zeb put down the top of the buggy and invited the Wizard to ride with them. The seat was amply wide enough for the little man and the two children, and when Jim started to leave the hall the kitten jumped upon his back and sat there quite contentedly.

So the procession moved through the streets, the bearers of the Sorcerer first, the Prince next, then Jim drawing the buggy with the strangers inside of it, and last the crowd of vegetable people who had no hearts and could neither smile nor frown.

The glass city had several fine streets, for a good many people lived there; but when the procession had passed through these it came upon a broad plain covered with gardens and watered by many pretty brooks that flowed through it. There were paths through these gardens, and over some of the brooks were ornamental glass bridges.

Dorothy and Zeb now got out of the buggy and walked beside the Prince, so that they might see and examine the flowers and plants better.

"Who built these lovely bridges?" asked the little girl.

"No one built them," answered the man with the star. "They grow."

"That's queer," said she. "Did the glass houses in your city grow, too?"

"Of course," he replied. "But it took a good many years for them to grow as large and fine as they are now. That is why we are so angry when a Rain of Stones comes to break our towers and crack our roofs."

"Can't you mend them?" she inquired.

"No; but they will grow together again, in time, and we must wait until they do."

They first passed through many beautiful gardens of flowers, which grew nearest the city; but Dorothy could hardly tell what kind of flowers they were, because the colors were constantly changing under the shifting lights of the six suns. A flower would be pink one second, white the next, then blue or yellow; and it was the same way when they came to the plants, which had broad leaves and grew close to the ground.

When they passed over a field of grass, Jim immediately stretched down his head and began to nibble.

"A nice country this is," he grumbled, "where a respectable horse has to eat pink grass!"

"It's violet," said the Wizard, who was in the buggy.

"Now it's blue," complained the horse. "As a matter of fact, I'm eating rainbow grass."

"How does it taste?" asked the Wizard.

"Not bad at all," said Jim. "If they give me plenty of it, I'll not complain about its color."

By this time the party had reached a freshly plowed field, and the Prince said to Dorothy:

"This is our planting ground."

Several Mangaboos came forward with glass spades and dug a hole in the ground. Then they put the two halves of the Sorcerer into it and covered him up. After that, other people brought water from a brook and sprinkled the earth.

"He will sprout very soon," said the Prince, "and grow into a large bush, from which we shall in time be able to pick several very good sorcerers."

"Do all your people grow on bushes?" asked the boy.

"Certainly," was the reply. "Do not all people grow upon bushes where you came from, on the outside of the earth?"

"Not that I ever heard of."

"How strange! But if you will come with me to one of our folk gardens I will show you the way we grow in the Land of the Mangaboos."

It appeared that these odd people, while they were able to walk through the air with ease, usually moved upon the ground in the ordinary way. There were no stairs in their houses, because they did not need them, but on a level surface they generally walked just as we do.

The little party of strangers now followed the Prince across a few more of the glass bridges and along several paths until they came to a garden enclosed by a high hedge. Jim had refused to leave the field of grass, where he was engaged in busily eating; so the Wizard got out of the buggy and joined Zeb and Dorothy, and the kitten followed demurely at their heels.

Inside the hedge they came upon row after row of large and handsome plants with broad leaves gracefully curving until their points nearly reached the ground. In the center of each plant grew a daintily dressed Mangaboo, for the clothing of all these creatures grew upon them and was attached to their bodies.

The growing Mangaboos were of all sizes, from the blossom that had just turned into a wee baby to the full-grown and almost-ripe man or woman. On some of the bushes might be seen a bud, a blossom, a baby, a half-grown person and a ripe one; but even those ready to pluck were motionless and silent, as if devoid of life. This sight explained to Dorothy why she had seen no children among the Mangaboos, a thing she had until now been unable to account for.

"Our people do not acquire their real life until they leave their bushes," said the Prince. "You will notice they are all attached to the plants by the soles of their feet, and when they are quite ripe they are easily separated from the stems and at once attain the powers of motion and speech. So while they grow they cannot be said to really live, and they must be picked before they can become good citizens."

"How long do you live, after you are picked?" asked Dorothy.

"That depends upon the care we take of ourselves," he replied. "If we keep cool and moist, and meet with no accidents, we often live for five years. I've been picked over six years, but our family is known to be especially long-lived."

"Do you eat?" asked the boy.

"Eat! No, indeed. We are quite solid inside our bodies, and have no need to eat, any more than does a potato."

"But the potatoes sometimes sprout," said Zeb.

"And sometimes we do," answered the Prince; "But that is considered a great misfortune, for then we must be planted at once."

"Where did you grow?" asked the Wizard.

"I will show you," was the reply. "Step this way, please."

He led them within another but smaller circle of hedge, where grew one large and beautiful bush.

"This," said he, "is the Royal Bush of the Mangaboos. All of our Princes and Rulers have grown upon this one bush from time immemorial."

They stood before it in silent admiration. On the central stalk stood poised the figure of a girl so exquisitely formed and colored and so lovely in the expression of her delicate features that Dorothy thought she had never seen so sweet and adorable a creature in all her life. The maiden's gown was soft as satin and fell about her in ample folds, while dainty lace-like traceries trimmed the bodice and sleeves. Her flesh was fine and smooth as polished ivory, and her poise expressed both dignity and grace.

"Who is this?" asked the Wizard curiously.

The Prince had been staring hard at the girl on the bush. Now he answered, with a touch of uneasiness in his cold tones:

"She is the Ruler destined to be my successor, for she is a Royal Princess. When she becomes fully ripe I must abandon the sovereignty of the Mangaboos to her."

"Isn't she ripe now?" asked Dorothy.

He hesitated.

"Not quite," said he, finally. "It will be several days before she needs to be picked, or at least that is my judgment. I am in no hurry to resign my office and be planted, you may be sure."

"Probably not," declared the Wizard, nodding.

"This is one of the most unpleasant things about our vegetable lives," continued the Prince with a sigh, "that while we are in our full prime we must give way to another, and be covered up in the ground to sprout and grow and give birth to other people."

"I'm sure the Princess is ready to be picked," asserted Dorothy, gazing hard at the beautiful girl on the bush. "She's as perfect as she can be."

"Never mind," answered the Prince, hastily, "she will be all right for a few days longer, and it is best for me to rule until I can dispose of you strangers, who have come to our land uninvited and must be attended to at once."

"What are you going to do with us?" asked Zeb.

"That is a matter I have not quite decided upon," was the reply. "I think I shall keep this Wizard until a new Sorcerer is ready to pick, for he seems quite skillful and may be of use to us. But the rest of you must be destroyed in some way, and you cannot be planted, because I do not wish horses and cats and meat people growing all over our country."

"You needn't worry," said Dorothy. "We wouldn't grow underground, I'm sure."

"But why destroy my friends?" asked the little Wizard. "Why not let them live?"

"They do not belong here," returned the Prince. "They have no right to be inside the earth at all."

"We didn't ask to come down here; we fell," said Dorothy.

"That is no excuse," declared the Prince coldly.

The children looked at each other in perplexity, and the Wizard sighed. Eureka rubbed her paw on her face and said in her soft, purring voice:

"He won't need to destroy *me*, for if I don't get something to eat pretty soon I shall starve to death, and so save him the trouble."

"If he planted you, he might grow some cat-tails," suggested the Wizard.

"Oh, Eureka! Perhaps we can find you some milkweeds to eat," said the boy.

"Phoo!" snarled the kitten; "I wouldn't touch the nasty things!"

"You don't need milk, Eureka," remarked Dorothy. "You are big enough now to eat any kind of food."

"If I can get it," added Eureka.

"I'm hungry myself," said Zeb. "But I noticed some strawberries growing in one of the gardens, and some melons in another place. These people don't eat such things, so, perhaps on our way back they will let us get them."

"Never mind your hunger," interrupted the Prince. "I shall order you destroyed in a few minutes, so you will have no need to ruin our pretty melon vines and berry bushes. Follow me, please, to meet your doom."

Chapter 5

Dorothy Picks the Princess

The words of the cold and moist vegetable Prince were not very comforting, and as he spoke them he turned away and left the enclosure. The children, feeling sad and despondent, were about to follow him when the Wizard touched Dorothy softly on her shoulder.

"Wait!" he whispered.

"What for?" asked the girl.

"Suppose we pick the Royal Princess," said the Wizard. "I'm quite sure she's ripe, and as soon as she comes to life she will be the Ruler, and may treat us better than that heartless Prince intends to."

"All right!" exclaimed Dorothy, eagerly. "Let's pick her while we have the chance, before the man with the star comes back."

So together they leaned over the great bush and each of them seized one hand of the lovely Princess.

"Pull!" cried Dorothy, and as they did so the royal lady leaned toward them and the stems snapped and separated from her feet. She was not at all heavy, so the Wizard and Dorothy managed to lift her gently to the ground.

The beautiful creature passed her hands over her eyes an instant, tucked in a stray lock of hair that had become disarranged, and after a look around the garden, made those present a gracious bow and said in a sweet but even-toned voice:

"I thank you very much."

"We salute your Royal Highness!" cried the Wizard, kneeling and kissing her hand.

Just then the voice of the Prince was heard calling upon them to hasten, and a moment later he returned to the enclosure, followed by a number of his people.

Instantly the Princess turned and faced him, and when he saw that she was picked the Prince stood still and began to tremble.

"Sir," said the Royal Lady with much dignity, "you have wronged me greatly, and would have wronged me still more had not these strangers come to my rescue. I have been ready for picking all the past week, but because you were selfish and desired to continue your unlawful rule, you left me to stand silent upon my bush.''

''I did not know that you were ripe,'' answered the Prince, in a low voice.

''Give me the Star of Royalty!'' she commanded.

Slowly he took the shining star from his own brow and placed it upon that of the Princess. Then all the people bowed low to her, and the Prince turned and walked away alone. What became of him afterward our friends never knew.

The people of Mangaboo now formed themselves into a procession and marched toward the glass city to escort their new ruler to her palace and to perform those ceremonies proper to the occasion. But while the people in the procession walked upon the ground the Princess walked in the air just above their heads, to show that she was a superior being and more exalted than her subjects.

No one now seemed to pay any attention to the strangers, so Dorothy and Zeb and the Wizard let the train pass on and then wandered by themselves into the vegetable gardens. They did not bother to cross the bridges over the brooks, but when they came to a stream they stepped high and walked in the air to the other side. This was a very interesting experience to them, and Dorothy said:

''I wonder why it is that we can walk so easily in the air.''

''Perhaps,'' answered the Wizard, ''it is because we are close to the center of the earth, where the attraction of gravitation is very slight. But I've noticed that many queer things happen in fairy countries."

"Is this a fairy country?" asked the boy.

"Of course it is," returned Dorothy promptly. "Only a fairy country could have veg'table people; and only in a fairy country could Eureka and Jim talk as we do."

"That's true," said Zeb thoughtfully.

In the vegetable gardens they found the strawberries and melons, and several other unknown but delicious fruits, of which they ate heartily. But the kitten bothered them constantly by demanding milk or meat, and called the Wizard names because he could not bring her a dish of milk by means of his magical arts.

As they sat upon the grass watching Jim, who was still busily eating, Eureka said:

"I don't believe you are a Wizard at all!"

"No," answered the little man, "you are quite right. In the strict sense of the word I am not a Wizard, but only a humbug."

"The Wizard of Oz has always been a humbug," agreed Dorothy. "I've known him for a long time."

"If that is so," said the boy, "how could he do that wonderful trick with the nine tiny piglets?"

"Don't know," said Dorothy, "but it must have been humbug."

"Very true," declared the Wizard, nodding at her. "It was necessary to deceive that ugly Sorcerer and the Prince, as well as their stupid people; but I don't mind telling you, who are my friends, that the thing was only a trick."

"But I saw the little pigs with my own eyes!" exclaimed Zeb.

"So did I," purred the kitten.

"To be sure," answered the Wizard. "You saw them because they were there. They are in my inside pocket now. But the pulling of them apart and pushing them together again was only a sleight-of-hand trick."

"Let's see the pigs," said Eureka, eagerly.

The little man felt carefully in his pocket and pulled out the tiny piglets, setting them upon the grass one by one, where they ran around and nibbled the tender blades.

"They're hungry, too," he said.

"Oh, what cunning things!" cried Dorothy, catching up one and petting it.

"Be careful!" said the piglet with a squeal. "You're squeezing me!"

"Dear me!" murmured the Wizard, looking at his pets in astonishment. "They can actually talk!"

"May I eat one of them?" asked the kitten, in a pleading voice. "I'm awfully hungry."

"Why, Eureka," said Dorothy, reproachfully, "what a cruel question! It would be dreadful to eat these dear little things."

"I should say so!" grunted another of the piglets, looking uneasily at the kitten. "Cats are cruel things."

"I'm not cruel," replied the kitten, yawning. "I'm just hungry."

"You cannot eat my piglets, even if you are starving," declared the little man in a stern voice. "They are the only things I have to prove I'm a wizard."

"How did they happen to be so little?" asked Dorothy. "I never saw such small pigs before."

"They are from the Island of Teenty-Weent," said the Wizard, "where everything is small because it's a small island. A sailor brought them to Los Angeles and I gave him nine tickets to the circus for them."

"But what am I going to eat?" wailed the kitten, sitting in front of Dorothy and looking pleadingly into her face. "There are no cows here to give milk; or any mice, or even grasshoppers. And if I can't eat the piglets you may as well plant me at once and raise catsup."

"I have an idea," said the Wizard, "that there are fishes in these brooks. Do you like fish?"

"Fish!" cried the kitten. "Do I like fish? Why, they're better than piglets—or even milk!"

"Then I'll try to catch you some," said he.

"But won't they be veg'table, like everything else here?" asked the kitten.

"I think not. Fishes are not animals, and they are as cold and moist as the vegetables themselves. There is no reason, that I can see, why they may not exist in the waters of this strange country."

Then the Wizard bent a pin for a hook and took a long piece of string from his pocket for a fish-line. The only bait he could find was a bright red blossom from a flower; but he knew fishes are easy to fool if anything bright attracts their attention, so he decided to try the blossom. Having thrown the end of his line in the water of a nearby brook he soon felt a sharp tug that told him a fish had bitten and was caught on the bent pin; so the little man drew in the string and, sure enough, the fish came with it and was landed safely on the shore, where it began to flop around in great excitement.

The fish was fat and round, and its scales glistened like beautifully cut jewels set close together; but there was no time to examine it closely, for Eureka made a jump and caught it between her claws, and in a few moments it had entirely disappeared.

"Oh, Eureka!" cried Dorothy. "Did you eat the bones?"

"If it had any bones, I ate them," replied the kitten composedly, as it washed its face after the meal. "But I don't think that fish had any bones, because I didn't feel them scratch my throat."

"You were very greedy," said the girl.

"I was very hungry," replied the kitten.

The little pigs had stood huddled in a group, watching this scene with frightened eyes.

"Cats are dreadful creatures!" said one of them.

"I'm glad we are not fishes!" said another.

"Don't worry," Dorothy murmured soothingly, "I'll not let the kitten hurt you."

Then she happened to remember that in a corner of her suitcase were one or two crackers that were left over from her luncheon on the train, and she went to the buggy and brought them. Eureka stuck up her nose at such food, but the tiny piglets squealed delightedly at the sight of the crackers and ate them up in a jiffy.

"Now let us go back to the city," suggested the Wizard. "That is, if Jim has had enough of the pink grass."

The cab-horse, who was browsing near, lifted

his head with a sigh.

"I've tried to eat a lot while I had the chance," said he, "for it's likely to be a long while between meals in this strange country. But I'm ready to go now, at any time you wish."

So, after the Wizard had put the piglets back into his inside pocket, where they cuddled up and went to sleep, the three climbed into the buggy and Jim started back to the town.

"Where shall we stay?" asked the girl.

"I think I shall take possession of the House of the Sorcerer," replied the Wizard. "For the Prince said in the presence of his people that he would keep me until they picked another Sorcerer, and the new Princess won't know but that we belong there."

They agreed to this plan, and when they reached the great square Jim drew the buggy into the big door of the domed hall.

"It doesn't look very homelike," said Dorothy, gazing around at the bare room. "But it's a place to stay, anyhow."

"What are those holes up there?" inquired the boy, pointing to some openings that appeared near the top of the dome.

"They look like doorways," said Dorothy. "Only there are no stairs to get to them."

"You forget that stairs are unnecessary," observed the Wizard. "Let us walk up, and see where the doors lead to."

With this he began walking in the air toward the high openings, and Dorothy and Zeb followed him. It was the same sort of climb one experiences when walking up a hill, and they were nearly out of breath when they came to the row of openings, which they perceived to be doorways leading into halls in the upper part of the house. Following these halls they discovered many small rooms opening from them, and some were furnished with glass benches, tables and chairs. But there were no beds at all.

"I wonder if these people never sleep," said the girl.

"Why, there seems to be no night at all in this country," Zeb replied. "Those colored suns are exactly in the same place they were when we came, and if there is no sunset there can be no night."

"Very true," agreed the Wizard. "But it is a long time since I have had any sleep, and I'm tired. So I think I shall lie down upon one of these hard glass benches and take a nap."

"I will, too," said Dorothy, and chose a little room at the end of the hall.

Zeb walked down again to unharness Jim, who, when he found himself free, rolled over a few times and then settled down to sleep, with Eureka nestling comfortably beside his big, bony body. Then the boy returned to one of the upper rooms, and in spite of the hardness of the glass bench was soon deep in slumberland.

Chapter 6

The Mangaboos Prove Dangerous

When the Wizard awoke, the six colored suns were shining down upon the Land of the Mangaboos just as they had done ever since his arrival. The little man, having had a good sleep, felt rested and refreshed, and looking through the glass partition of the room he saw Zeb sitting up on his bench and yawning. So the Wizard went in to him.

"Zeb," said he, "my balloon is of no further use in this strange country, so I may as well leave it on the square where it fell. But in the basket-car are some things I would like to keep with me. I wish you would go and fetch my satchel, two lanterns, and a can of kerosene oil that is under the seat. There is nothing else that I care about."

So the boy went willingly upon the errand, and by the time he had returned Dorothy was awake. Then the three held a counsel to decide what they should do next, but could think of no way to better their condition.

"I don't like these veg'table people," said the little girl. "They're cold and flabby, like cabbages, in spite of their prettiness."

"I agree with you. It is because there is no warm blood in them," remarked the Wizard.

"And they have no hearts; so they can't love anyone—not even themselves," declared the boy.

"The Princess is lovely to look at," continued Dorothy thoughtfully, "but I don't care much for her, after all. If there was any other place to go, I'd like to go there."

"But *is* there any other place?" asked the Wizard.

"I don't know," she answered.

Just then they heard the big voice of Jim the cab-horse calling to them. Going to the doorway leading to the dome, they found the Princess and a throng of her people had entered the House of the Sorcerer.

So they went down to greet the beautiful vegetable lady, who said to them:

"I have been talking with my advisors about you meat people, and we have decided that you do not belong in the Land of the Mangaboos and must not remain here."

"How can we go away?" asked Dorothy.

"Oh, you cannot go away, of course; so you must be destroyed," was the answer.

"In what way?" inquired the Wizard.

"We shall throw you three people into the Garden of the Twining Vines," said the Princess, "and they will soon crush you and devour your bodies to make themselves grow bigger. The animals you have with you we will drive to the mountains and put into the Black Pit. Then our country will be rid of all its unwelcome visitors."

"But you are in need of a Sorcerer," said the Wizard, "and not one of those growing is yet ripe enough to pick. I am greater than any thorn-covered sorcerer that ever grew in your garden. Why destroy me?"

"It is true we need a Sorcerer," acknowledged the Princess, "but I am informed that one of our own will be ready to pick in a few days, to take the place of Gwig, whom you cut in two before it was time for him to be planted. Let us see your arts, and the sorceries you are able to perform. Then I will decide whether to destroy you with the others or not."

At this the Wizard made a bow to the people and repeated his trick of producing the nine tiny piglets and making them disappear again. He did it very cleverly, indeed, and the Princess looked at the strange piglets as if she were as truly astonished as any vegetable person could be. But afterward she said:

"I have heard of this wonderful magic. But it accomplishes nothing of value. What else can you do?"

The Wizard tried to think. Then he jointed together the blades of his sword and balanced it very skillfully upon the end of his nose. But even that did not satisfy the Princess.

Just then his eye fell upon the lanterns and the can of kerosene oil which Zeb had brought from the car of his balloon, and he got a clever idea from those commonplace things.

"Your Highness," said he, "I will now proceed to prove my magic by creating two suns that you have never seen before; also I will exhibit a Destroyer much more dreadful than your Clinging Vines."

So he placed Dorothy upon one side of him and the boy upon the other and set a lantern upon each of their heads.

"Don't laugh," he whispered to them, "or you will spoil the effect of my magic."

Then, with much dignity and a look of vast importance upon his wrinkled face, the Wizard got out his matchbox and lighted the two lanterns. The glare they made was very small when compared with the radiance of the six great colored suns; but still they gleamed steadily and clearly. The Mangaboos were much impressed because they had never before seen any light that did not come directly from their suns.

Next the Wizard poured a pool of oil from the can upon the glass floor, where it covered quite a broad surface. When he lighted the oil a hundred tongues of flame shot up, and the effect was really imposing.

"Now, Princess," exclaimed the Wizard, "those of your advisors who wished to throw us into the Garden of Clinging Vines must step within this circle of light. If they advised you well, and were in the right, they will not be injured in any way. But if any advised you wrongly, the light will wither him."

The advisors of the Princess did not like this test; but she commanded them to step into the flame and one by one they did so, and were scorched so badly that the air was soon filled with an odor like that of baked potatoes. Some of the Mangaboos fell down and had to be dragged from the fire, and all were so withered that it would be necessary to plant them at once.

"Sir," said the Princess to the Wizard, "you are greater than any Sorcerer we have ever known. As it is evident that my people have advised me wrongly, I will not cast you three people into the dreadful Garden of the Clinging Vines; but your animals must be driven into the Black Pit in the mountain, for my subjects cannot bear to have them around."

The Wizard was so pleased to have saved the two children and himself that he said nothing against this decree. But when the Princess had gone both Jim and Eureka protested they did not want to go to the Black Pit, and Dorothy promised she would do all that she could to save them from such a fate.

For two or three days after this—if we call days the periods between sleep, there being no night to divide the hours into days—our friends were not disturbed in any way. They were even permitted to occupy the House of the Sorcerer in peace, as if it had been their own, and to wander in the gardens in search of food.

Once they came near to the enclosed Garden of the Clinging Vines and, walking high into the air, looked down upon it with much interest. They saw a mass of tough green vines all matted together and writhing and twisting around like a nest of great snakes. Everything the vines touched they crushed, and our adventurers were indeed thankful to have escaped being cast among them.

Whenever the Wizard went to sleep he would take the nine tiny piglets from his pocket and let them run around on the floor of his room to amuse themselves and get some exercise; and one time they found his glass door ajar and wandered into the hall and then into the bottom part of the great dome, walking through the air as easily as Eureka could. They knew the kitten, by this time, so they scampered over to where she lay beside Jim and commenced to frisk and play with her.

The cab-horse, who never slept long at a time, sat upon his haunches and watched the tiny piglets and the kitten with much approval.

"Don't be rough!" he would call out, if Eureka knocked over one of the round, fat piglets with her paw; but the pigs never minded, and enjoyed the sport very greatly.

Suddenly they looked up to find the room filled with the silent, solemn-eyed Mangaboos. Each of the vegetable folks bore a branch covered with sharp thorns, which was thrust defiantly toward the horse, the kitten and the piglets.

"Here—stop this foolishness!" Jim roared, angrily; but after being pricked once or twice he got upon his four legs and kept out of the way of the thorns.

The Mangaboos surrounded them in solid ranks, but left an opening to the doorway of the hall; so the animals slowly retreated until they were driven from the room and out upon the street. Here were more of the vegetable people with thorns, and silently they urged the now frightened creatures down the street. Jim had to be careful not to step upon the tiny piglets, who scampered under his feet grunting and squealing, while Eureka, snarling and biting at the thorns pushed toward her, also tried to protect the pretty little things from injury. Slowly but steadily the heartless Mangaboos drove them on, until they had passed through the city and the gardens and come to the broad plains leading to the mountain.

"What does all this mean, anyhow?" asked the horse, jumping to escape a thorn.

"Why, they are driving us toward the Black Pit, into which they threatened to cast us," replied the kitten. "If I were as big as you are, Jim, I'd fight these miserable turnip roots!"

"What would you do?" inquired Jim.

"I'd kick out with those long legs and iron-shod hoofs."

"All right," said the horse. "I'll do it."

An instant later he suddenly backed toward the crowd of Mangaboos and kicked out his hind legs as hard as he could. A dozen of them smashed together and tumbled to the ground, and seeing his success Jim kicked again and again, charging into the vegetable crowd, knocking them in all directions and sending the others scattering to escape his iron heels. Eureka helped him by flying into the faces of the enemy and scratching and biting furiously, and the kitten ruined so many vegetable complexions that the Mangaboos feared her as much as they did the horse.

But the foes were too many to be repulsed

for long. They tired Jim and Eureka out, and although the field of battle was thickly covered with mashed and disabled Mangaboos, our animal friends had to give up at last and allow themselves to be driven to the mountain.

Chapter 7

Into the Black Pit
and Out Again

When they came to the mountain it proved to be
a rugged, towering chunk of deep green glass,
and looked dismal and forbidding in the
extreme. Halfway up the steep was a yawning
cave, black as night beyond the point where the
rainbow rays of the colored suns reached into
it.

The Mangaboos drove the horse and the
kitten and the piglets into this dark hole and
then, having pushed the buggy in after them—
for it seemed some of them had dragged it all the
way from the domed hall—they began to pile
big glass rocks within the entrance, so that the
prisoners could not get out again.

"This is dreadful!" groaned Jim. "It will be
about the end of our adventures, I guess."

"If the Wizard was here," said one of the
piglets, sobbing bitterly, "he would not see us
suffer so."

"We ought to have called him and Dorothy when we were first attacked," added Eureka. "But never mind; be brave, my friends, and I will go and tell our masters where you are, and get them to come to your rescue."

The mouth of the hole was nearly filled up now, but the kitten gave a leap through the remaining opening and at once scampered up into the air. The Mangaboos saw her escape, and several of them caught up their thorns and gave chase, mounting through the air after her. Eureka, however, was lighter than the Mangaboos, and while they could mount only about a hundred feet above the earth the kitten found she could go nearly two hundred feet. So she ran along over their heads until she had left them far behind and below and had come to the city and the House of the Sorcerer. There she entered in at Dorothy's window in the dome and aroused her from her sleep.

As soon as the little girl knew what had happened she awakened the Wizard and Zeb, and at once preparations were made to go to the rescue of Jim and the piglets. The Wizard carried his satchel, which was quite heavy, and Zeb carried the two lanterns and the oil can. Dorothy's wicker suitcase was still under the seat of the buggy, and by good fortune the boy had also placed the harness in the buggy when he had taken it off from Jim to let the horse lie down and rest. So there was nothing for the girl to carry but the kitten, which she held close to her bosom and tried to comfort, for its little heart was still beating rapidly.

Some of the Mangaboos discovered them as soon as they left the House of the Sorcerer; but when they started toward the mountain the vegetable people allowed them to proceed without interference, yet followed in a crowd behind them so that they could not go back again.

Before long they neared the Black Pit, where a busy swarm of Mangaboos, headed by their Princess, was engaged in piling up glass rocks before the entrance.

"Stop, I command you!" cried the Wizard, in an angry tone, and at once began pulling down the rocks to liberate Jim and the piglets. Instead of opposing him in this they stood back in silence until he had made a good-sized hole in the barrier, when by order of the Princess they all sprang forward and thrust out their sharp thorns.

Dorothy hopped inside the opening to escape being pricked, and Zeb and the Wizard, after enduring a few stabs from the thorns, were glad to follow her. At once the Mangaboos began piling up the rocks of glass again, and as the little man realized that they were all about to be entombed in the mountain he said to the children:

"My dears, what shall we do? Jump out and fight?"

"What's the use?" replied Dorothy. "I'd as soon die here as live much longer among those cruel and heartless people."

"That's the way I feel about it," remarked Zeb, rubbing his wounds. "I've had enough of the Mangaboos."

"All right," said the Wizard. "I'm with you, whatever you decide. But we can't live long in this cavern, that's certain."

Noticing that the light was growing dim he picked up his nine piglets, patted each one lovingly on its fat little head, and placed them carefully in his inside pocket.

Zeb struck a match and lighted one of the lanterns. The rays of the colored suns were now shut out from them forever, for the last chinks had been filled up in the wall that separated their prison from the Land of the Mangaboos.

"How big is this hole?" asked Dorothy.

"I'll explore it and see," replied the boy.

So he carried the lantern back for quite a distance, while Dorothy and the Wizard followed at his side. The cavern did not come to an end, as they had expected it would, but slanted upward through the great glass mountain, running in a direction that promised to lead them to the side opposite the Mangaboo country.

"It isn't a bad road," observed the Wizard, "and if we followed it it might lead us to some place that is more comfortable than this black pocket we are now in. I suppose the vegetable folk were always afraid to enter this cavern because it is dark; but we have our lanterns to light the way, so I propose that we start out and discover where this tunnel in the mountain leads to."

The others agreed readily to this sensible suggestion, and at once the boy began to harness Jim to the buggy. When all was in readiness the three took their seats in the buggy and Jim started cautiously along the way, Zeb driving while the

Wizard and Dorothy each held a lighted lantern so the horse could see where to go.

Sometimes the tunnel was so narrow that the wheels of the buggy grazed the sides; then it would broaden out as wide as a street. But the floor was usually smooth, and for a long time they traveled on without any accident. Jim stopped sometimes to rest, for the climb was rather steep and tiresome.

"We must be nearly as high as the six colored suns, by this time," said Dorothy. "I didn't know this mountain was so tall."

"We are certainly a good distance away from the Land of the Mangaboos," added Zeb, "for we have slanted away from it ever since we started."

But they kept steadily moving, and just as Jim was about tired out with his long journey the way suddenly grew lighter, and Zeb put out the lanterns to save the oil.

To their joy they found it was a white light that now greeted them, for all were weary of the colored rainbow lights which, after a time, had made their eyes ache with their constantly shifting rays. The sides of the tunnel showed before them like the inside of a long spyglass, and the floor became more level. Jim hastened his lagging steps at this assurance of a quick relief from the dark passage, and in a few moments more they had emerged from the mountain and found themselves face to face with a new and charming country.

Chapter 8
The Valley of Voices

By journeying through the glass mountain they
had reached a delightful valley that was shaped
like the hollow of a great cup, with another
rugged mountain showing on the other side of
it, and soft and pretty green hills at the ends.
It was all laid out into lovely lawns and
gardens, with pebble paths leading through
them and groves of beautiful and stately trees
dotting the landscape here and there. There
were orchards, too, bearing luscious fruits that
are all unknown in our world. Alluring brooks
of crystal water flowed sparkling between their
flower-strewn banks, while scattered over the
valley were dozens of the quaintest and most
picturesque cottages our travelers had ever
beheld. None of them were in clusters, such as
villages or towns, but each had ample grounds
of its own, with orchards and gardens surrounding it.

As the new arrivals gazed upon this exquisite scene they were enraptured by its beauties and the fragrance that permeated the soft air, which they breathed so gratefully after the confined atmosphere of the tunnel. Several minutes were consumed in silent admiration before they noticed two very singular and unusual facts about this valley. One was that it was lighted from some unseen source; for no sun or moon was in the arched blue sky, although every object was flooded with a clear and perfect light. The second and even more singular fact was the absence of any inhabitant of this splendid place. From their elevated position they could overlook the entire valley, but not a single moving object could they see. All appeared mysteriously deserted.

The mountain on this side was not glass, but made of a stone similar to granite. With some difficulty and danger Jim drew the buggy over the loose rocks until he reached the green lawns below, where the paths and orchards and gardens began. The nearest cottage was still some distance away.

"Isn't it fine?" cried Dorothy, in a joyous voice, as she sprang out of the buggy and let Eureka run frolicking over the velvety grass.

"Yes, indeed!" answered Zeb. "We were lucky to get away from those dreadful vegetable people."

"It wouldn't be so bad," remarked the Wizard, gazing around him, "if we were obliged to live here always. We couldn't find a prettier place, I'm sure."

He took the piglets from his pocket and let them run on the grass, and Jim tasted a mouthful of the green blades and declared he was very contented in his new surroundings.

"We can't walk in the air here, though," called Eureka, who had tried it and failed; but the others were satisfied to walk on the ground, and the Wizard said they must be nearer the surface of the earth than they had been in the Mangaboo country, for everything was more homelike and natural.

"But where are the people?" asked Dorothy.

The little man shook his bald head.

"Can't imagine, my dear," he replied.

They heard the sudden twittering of a bird, but could not find the creature anywhere. Slowly they walked along the path toward the nearest cottage, the piglets racing and gamboling beside them and Jim pausing at every step for another mouthful of grass.

Presently they came to a low plant which had broad, spreading leaves; in the center of each grew a single fruit about as large as a peach. The fruit was so daintily colored and so fragrant, and looked so appetizing and delicious that Dorothy stopped and exclaimed:

"What is it, do you s'pose?"

The piglets had smelled the fruit quickly, and before the girl could reach out her hand to pluck it every one of the nine tiny ones had rushed in and commenced to devour it with great eagerness.

"It's good, anyway," said Zeb, "or those little rascals wouldn't have gobbled it up so greedily."

"Where are they?" asked Dorothy, in astonishment.

They all looked around, but the piglets had disappeared.

"Dear me!" cried the Wizard. "They must have run away. But I didn't see them go; did you?"

"No!" replied the boy and the girl together.

"Here—piggy, piggy, piggy!" called their master anxiously.

Several squeals and grunts were instantly heard at his feet, but the Wizard could not discover a single piglet.

"Where are you?" he asked.

"Why, right beside you," spoke a tiny voice. "Can't you see us?"

"No," answered the little man in a puzzled tone.

"We can see you," said another of the piglets.

The Wizard stooped down and put out his hand, and at once felt the small fat body of one of his pets. He picked it up, but could not see what he held.

"It is very strange," said he soberly. "The piglets have become invisible, in some curious way."

"I'll bet it's because they ate that peach!" cried the kitten.

"It wasn't a peach, Eureka," said Dorothy. "I only hope it wasn't poison."

"It was fine, Dorothy," called one of the piglets.

"We'll eat all we can find of them," said another.

"But *we* mus'n't eat them," the Wizard warned the children, "or we too may become invisible and lose each other. If we come across another of the strange fruit we must avoid it."

Calling the piglets to him he picked them all up, one by one, and put them away in his pocket; for although he could not see them he could feel them, and when he had buttoned his coat he knew they were safe for the present.

The travelers now resumed their walk toward the cottage, which they presently reached. It was a pretty place, with vines growing thickly over the broad front porch. The door stood open and a table was set in the front room, with four chairs drawn up to it. On the table were plates, knives and forks, and dishes of bread, meat and fruits. The meat was smoking hot and the knives and forks were performing strange antics and jumping here and there in quite a puzzling way. But not a single person appeared to be in the room.

"How funny!" exclaimed Dorothy, who with Zeb and the Wizard now stood in the doorway.

A peal of merry laughter answered her, and the knives and forks fell to the plates with a clatter. One of the chairs pushed back from the table, and this was so astonishing and mysterious that Dorothy was almost tempted to run away in fright.

"Here are strangers, mama!" cried the shrill and childish voice of some unseen person.

"So I see, my dear," answered another voice, soft and womanly.

"What do you want?" demanded a third voice in a stern, gruff accent.

"Well, well!" said the Wizard, "are there really people in this room?"

"Of course," replied the man's voice.

"And—pardon me for the foolish question— but, are you all invisible?"

"Surely," the woman answered, repeating her low, rippling laughter. "Are you surprised that you are unable to see the people of Voe?"

"Why, yes," stammered the Wizard. "All the people I have ever met before were very plain to see."

"Where do you come from, then?" asked the woman, in a curious tone.

"We belong upon the face of the earth," explained the Wizard, "but recently, during an earthquake, we fell down a crack and landed in the Country of the Mangaboos."

"Dreadful creatures!" exclaimed the woman's voice. "I've heard of them."

"They walled us up in a mountain," continued the Wizard, "but we found there was a tunnel through to this side, so we came here. It is a beautiful place. What do you call it?"

"It is the Valley of Voe."

"Thank you. We have seen no people since we arrived, so we came to this house to inquire our way."

"Are you hungry?" asked the woman's voice.

"I could eat something," said Dorothy.

"So could I," added Zeb.

"But we do not wish to intrude, I assure you," the Wizard hastened to say.

"That's all right," returned the man's voice, more pleasantly than before. "You are welcome to what we have."

As he spoke the voice came so near to Zeb that he jumped back in alarm. Two childish voices laughed merrily at this action, and Dorothy was sure they were in no danger among such light-hearted folks, even if those folks couldn't be seen.

"What curious animal is that which is eating the grass on my lawn?" inquired the man's voice.

"That's Jim," said the girl. "He's a horse."

"What is he good for?" was the next question.

"He draws the buggy you see fastened to him, and we ride in the buggy instead of walking," she explained.

"Can he fight?" asked the man's voice.

"No! He can kick pretty hard with his heels, and bite a little; but Jim can't 'zactly fight," she replied.

"Then the bears will get him," said one of the children's voices.

"Bears!" exclaimed Dorothy. "Are there bears here?"

"That is the one evil of our country," answered the invisible man. "Many large and fierce bears roam in the Valley of Voe, and when they can catch any of us they eat us up; but as they cannot see us, we seldom get caught."

"Are the bears invis'ble, too?" asked the girl.

"Yes; for they eat of the dama-fruit, as we all do, and that keeps them from being seen by any eye, whether human or animal."

"Does the dama-fruit grow on a low bush, and look something like a peach?" asked the Wizard.

"Yes," was the reply.

"If it makes you invis'ble, why do you eat it?" Dorothy inquired.

"For two reasons, my dear," the woman's voice answered. "The dama-fruit is the most delicious thing that grows, and when it makes us invisible the bears cannot find us to eat us up. But now, good wanderers, your luncheon is on the table, so please sit down and eat as much as you like."

Chapter 9

They Fight the Invisible Bears

The strangers took their seats at the table willingly enough, for they were all hungry and the platters were now heaped with good things to eat. In front of each place was a plate bearing one of the delicious dama-fruit, and the perfume that rose from these was so enticing and sweet that they were sorely tempted to eat of them and become invisible.

But Dorothy satisfied her hunger with other things, and her companions did likewise, resisting the temptation.

"Why do you not eat the damas?" asked the woman's voice.

"We don't want to get invis'ble," answered the girl.

"But if you remain visible the bears will see you and devour you," said a girlish young voice, that belonged to one of the children. "We who live here much prefer to be invisible; for we can still hug and kiss one another, and are quite safe from the bears.''

''And we do not have to be so particular about our dress,'' remarked the man.

''And mama can't tell whether my face is dirty or not!'' added the other childish voice, gleefully.

''But I make you wash it, every time I think of it,'' said the mother. ''For it stands to reason your face is dirty, Ianu, whether I can see it or not.''

Dorothy laughed and stretched out her hands.

''Come here, please—Ianu and your sister—and let me feel of you,'' she requested.

They came to her willingly, and Dorothy passed her hands over their faces and forms and decided one was a girl of about her own age and the other a boy somewhat smaller. The girl's hair was soft and fluffy and her skin as smooth as satin. When Dorothy gently touched her nose and ears and lips they seemed to be well and delicately formed.

''If I could see you I am sure you would be beautiful,'' she declared.

The girl laughed, and her mother said:

''We are not vain in the Valley of Voe, because we cannot display our beauty, and good actions and pleasant ways are what make us lovely to our companions. Yet we can see and appreciate the beauties of nature, the dainty flowers and trees, the green fields and the clear blue of the sky.''

''How about the birds and beasts and fishes?'' asked Zeb.

"The birds we cannot see, because they love to eat of the damas as much as we do; yet we hear their sweet songs and enjoy them. Neither can we see the cruel bears, for they also eat the fruit. But the fishes that swim in our brooks we can see, and often we catch them to eat."

"It occurs to me you have a great deal to make you happy, even while invisible," remarked the Wizard. "Nevertheless, we prefer to remain visible while we are in your valley."

Just then Eureka came in, for she had been until now wandering outside with Jim; and when the kitten saw the table set with food she cried out:

"Now you must feed me, Dorothy, for I'm half starved."

The children were inclined to be frightened by the sight of the small animal, which reminded them of the bears; but Dorothy reassured them by explaining that Eureka was a pet and could do no harm even if she wished to. Then, as the others had by this time moved away from the table, the kitten sprang upon the chair and put her paws upon the cloth to see what there was to eat. To her surprise an unseen hand clutched her and held her suspended in the air. Eureka was frantic with terror, and tried to scratch and bite, so the next moment she was dropped to the floor.

"Did you see that, Dorothy?" she gasped.

"Yes, dear," her mistress replied; "there are people living in this house, although we cannot see them. And you must have better manners, Eureka, or something worse will happen to you."

She placed a plate of food upon the floor and the kitten ate greedily.

"Give me that nice-smelling fruit I saw on the table," she begged, when she had cleaned the plate.

"Those are damas," said Dorothy, "and you must never even taste them, Eureka, or you'll get invis'ble, and then we can't see you at all."

The kitten gazed wistfully at the forbidden fruit.

"Does it hurt to be invis'ble?" she asked.

"I don't know," Dorothy answered, "but it would hurt me dreadfully to lose you."

"Very well, I won't touch it," decided the kitten. "But you must keep it away from me, for the smell is very tempting."

"Can you tell us, sir or ma'am," said the Wizard, addressing the air because he did not quite know where the unseen people stood, "if there is any way we can get out of your beautiful Valley, and on top of the Earth again."

"Oh, one can leave the Valley easily enough," answered the man's voice, "but to do so you must enter a far less pleasant country. As for reaching the top of the earth, I have never heard that it is possible to do that, and if you succeeded in getting there you would probably fall off."

"Oh, no," said Dorothy, "we've been there, and we know."

"The Valley of Voe is certainly a charming place," resumed the Wizard, "but we cannot be contented in any other land than our own, for long. Even if we should come to unpleasant places on our way it is necessary, in order to reach the earth's surface, to keep moving on toward it."

"In that case," said the man, "it will be best for you to cross our Valley and mount the spiral staircase inside the Pyramid Mountain. The top of that mountain is lost in the clouds, and when you reach it you will be in the awful Land of Naught, where the Gargoyles live."

"What are Gargoyles?" asked Zeb.

"I do not know, young sir. Our greatest Champion, Overman-Anu, once climbed the spiral stairway and fought nine days with the Gargoyles before he could escape them and come back; but he could never be induced to describe the dreadful creatures, and soon afterward a bear caught him and ate him up."

The wanderers were rather discouraged by this gloomy report, but Dorothy said with a sigh:

"If the only way to get home is to meet the Gurgles, then we've got to meet 'em. They can't be worse than the Wicked Witch or the Nome King."

"But you must remember you had the Scarecrow and the Tin Woodman to help you conquer those enemies," suggested the Wizard. "Just now, my dear, there is not a single warrior in your company."

"Oh, I guess Zeb could fight if he had to. Couldn't you, Zeb?" asked the little girl.

"Perhaps; if I had to," answered Zeb doubtfully.

"And you have the jointed sword that you chopped the veg'table Sorcerer in two with," the girl said to the little man.

"True," he replied. "And in my satchel are other useful things to fight with."

"What the Gargoyles most dread is a noise," said the man's voice. "Our Champion told me that when he shouted his battle cry the creatures shuddered and drew back, hesitating to continue the combat. But they were in great numbers, and the Champion could not shout much because he had to save his breath for fighting."

"Very good," said the Wizard. "We can all yell better than we can fight, so we ought to defeat the Gargoyles."

"But tell me," said Dorothy, "how did such a brave Champion happen to let the bears eat him? And if he was invis'ble, and the bears invis'ble, who knows that they really ate him up?"

"The Champion had killed eleven bears in his time," returned the unseen man, "and we know this is true because when any creature is dead the invisible charm of the dama-fruit ceases to be active, and the slain one can be plainly seen by all eyes. When the Champion killed a bear everyone could see it; and when the bears killed the Champion we all saw several pieces of him scattered about, which of course disappeared again when the bears devoured them."

They now bade farewell to the kind but unseen people of the cottage, and after the man had called their attention to a high, pyramid-shaped mountain on the opposite side of the Valley, and told them how to travel in order to reach it, they again started upon their journey.

They followed the course of a broad stream and passed several more pretty cottages; but of course they saw no one, nor did anyone speak to them. Fruits and flowers grew plentifully all about, and there were many of the delicious damas that the people of Voe were so fond of.

About noon they stopped to allow Jim to rest in the shade of a pretty orchard, and while they plucked and ate some of the cherries and plums that grew there a soft voice suddenly said to them:

"There are bears nearby. Be careful."

The Wizard got out his sword at once, and Zeb grabbed the horsewhip. Dorothy climbed into the buggy, although Jim had been unharnessed from it and was grazing some distance away.

The owner of the unseen voice laughed lightly and said:

"You cannot escape the bears that way."

"How *can* we 'scape?" asked Dorothy nervously, for an unseen danger is always the hardest to face.

"You must take to the river," was the reply. "The bears will not venture upon the water."

"But we would be drowned!" exclaimed the girl.

"Oh, there is no need of that," said the voice, which from its gentle tones seemed to belong to a young girl. "You are strangers in the Valley of Voe, and do not seem to know our ways; so I will try to save you."

The next moment a broad-leaved plant was jerked from the ground where it grew and held suspended in the air before the Wizard.

"Sir," said the voice, "you must rub these leaves upon the soles of all your feet, and then you will be able to walk upon the water without sinking below the surface. It is a secret the bears do not know, and we people of Voe usually walk upon the water when we travel, and so escape our enemies."

"Thank you!" cried the Wizard joyfully, and at once rubbed a leaf upon the soles of Dorothy's shoes and then upon his own. The girl took a leaf and rubbed it upon the kitten's paws, and the rest of the plant was handed to Zeb, who, after applying it to his own feet, carefully rubbed it upon all four of Jim's hoofs and then upon the tires of the buggy wheels. He had nearly finished this last task when a low growling was suddenly heard and the horse began to jump around and kick viciously with his heels.

"Quick! To the water, or you are lost!" cried their unseen friend, and without hesitation the Wizard drew the buggy down the bank and out upon the broad river, for Dorothy was still seated in it with Eureka in her arms. They did not sink at all, owing to the virtues of the strange plant they had used, and when the buggy was in the middle of the stream the Wizard returned to the bank to assist Zeb and Jim.

The horse was plunging madly about, and two or three deep gashes appeared upon its flanks, from which the blood flowed freely.

"Run for the river!" shouted the Wizard, and Jim quickly freed himself from his unseen tormenters by a few vicious kicks and then obeyed. As soon as he trotted out upon the surface of the river he found himself safe from pursuit, and Zeb was already running across the water toward Dorothy.

As the little Wizard turned to follow them he felt a hot breath against his cheek and heard a low, fierce growl. At once he began stabbing at the air with his sword, and he knew that he had struck some substance because when he drew back the blade it was dripping with blood. The third time that he thrust out the weapon there was a loud roar and a fall, and suddenly at his feet appeared the form of a great red bear, which was nearly as big as the horse and much stronger and fiercer. The beast was quite dead from the sword thrusts, and after a glance at its terrible claws and sharp teeth the little man turned in a panic and rushed out upon the water, for other menacing growls told him more bears were near.

On the river, however, the adventurers seemed to be perfectly safe. Dorothy and the buggy had floated slowly down stream with the current of the water, and the others made haste to join her. The Wizard opened his satchel and got out some sticking-plaster with which he mended the cuts Jim had received from the claws of the bears.

"I think we'd better stick to the river, after this," said Dorothy. "If our unknown friend hadn't warned us, and told us what to do, we would all be dead by this time."

"That is true," agreed the Wizard, "and as the river seems to be flowing in the direction of the Pyramid Mountain it will be the easiest way for us to travel."

Zeb hitched Jim to the buggy again, and the horse trotted along and drew them rapidly over the smooth water. The kitten was at first dreadfully afraid of getting wet, but Dorothy let her down and soon Eureka was frisking along beside the buggy without being scared a bit. Once a little fish swam too near the surface, and the kitten grabbed it in her mouth and ate it up as quick as a wink; but Dorothy cautioned her to be careful what she ate in this valley of enchantments, and no more fishes were careless enough to swim within reach.

After a journey of several hours they came to a point where the river curved, and they found they must cross a mile or so of the Valley before they came to the Pyramid Mountain. There were few houses in this part, and few orchards or flowers; so our friends feared they might encounter more of the savage bears, which they had learned to dread with all their hearts.

"You'll have to make a dash, Jim," said the Wizard, "and run as fast as you can go."

"All right," answered the horse; "I'll do my best. But you must remember I'm old, and my dashing days are past and gone."

All three got into the buggy and Zeb picked up the reins, though Jim needed no guidance of any sort. The horse was still smarting from the sharp claws of the invisible bears, and as soon as he was on land and headed toward the mountain the thought that more of those fearsome creatures might be near acted as a spur and sent him galloping along in a way that made Dorothy catch her breath.

Then Zeb, in a spirit of mischief, uttered a growl like that of the bears, and Jim pricked up his ears and fairly flew. His bony legs moved so fast they could scarcely be seen, and the Wizard clung fast to the seat and yelled "Whoa!" at the top of his voice.

"I—I'm 'fraid he's—he's running away!" gasped Dorothy.

"I *know* he is," said Zeb. "But no bear can catch him if he keeps up that gait—and the harness or the buggy don't break."

Jim did not make a mile a minute; but almost before they were aware of it he drew up at the foot of the mountain, so suddenly that the Wizard and Zeb both sailed over the dashboard and landed in the soft grass—where they rolled over several times before they stopped. Dorothy nearly went with them, but she was holding fast to the iron rail of the seat, and that saved her. She squeezed the kitten, though, until it screeched; and then the old cab-horse made several curious sounds that led the little girl to suspect he was laughing at them all.

Chapter 10

The Braided Man of Pyramid Mountain

The mountain before them was shaped like a cone and was so tall that its point was lost in the clouds. Directly facing the place where Jim had stopped was an arched opening leading to a broad stairway. The stairs were cut in the rock inside the mountain, and they were broad and not very steep, because they circled around like a corkscrew, and at the arched opening where the flight began the circle was quite big. At the foot of the stairs was a sign reading:

WARNING.
These steps lead to the
Land of the Gargoyles.
DANGER! KEEP OUT.

"I wonder how Jim is ever going to draw the buggy up so many stairs," said Dorothy gravely.

"No trouble at all," declared the horse with a contemptuous neigh. "Still, I don't care to drag any passengers. You'll all have to walk."

"Suppose the stairs get steeper?" suggested Zeb doubtfully.

"Then you'll have to boost the buggy wheels, that's all," answered Jim.

"We'll try it, anyway," said the Wizard. "It's the only way to get out of the Valley of Voe."

So they began to ascend the stairs, Dorothy and the Wizard first, Jim next, drawing the buggy, and then Zeb to watch that nothing happened to the harness.

The light was dim, and soon they mounted into total darkness, so that the Wizard was obliged to get out his lanterns to light the way. But this enabled them to proceed steadily until they came to a landing where there was a rift in the side of the mountain that let in both light and air. Looking through this opening they could see the Valley of Voe lying far below them, the cottages seeming like toy houses from that distance.

After resting a few moments they resumed their climb, and still the stairs were broad and low enough for Jim to draw the buggy easily after him. The old horse panted a little, and had to stop often to get his breath. At such times they were all glad to wait for him, for continually climbing up stairs is sure to make one's legs ache.

They wound about, always going upward, for some time. The lights from the lanterns dimly showed the way, but it was a gloomy journey, and they were pleased when a broad streak of light ahead assured them they were coming to a second landing.

Here one side of the mountain had a great hole in it, like the mouth of a cavern, and the stairs stopped at the near edge of the floor and commenced ascending again at the opposite edge.

The opening in the mountain was on the side opposite to the Valley of Voe, and our travelers looked out upon a strange scene. Below them was a vast space, at the bottom of which was a black sea with rolling billows, through which little tongues of flame constantly shot up. Just above them, and almost on a level with their platform, were banks of rolling clouds which constantly shifted position and changed color. The blues and grays were very beautiful, and Dorothy noticed that on the cloud banks sat or reclined fleecy, shadowy forms of beautiful beings who must have been the Cloud Fairies. Mortals who stand upon the earth and look up at the sky cannot often distinguish these forms, but our friends were now so near to the clouds that they observed the dainty fairies very clearly.

"Are they real?" asked Zeb in an awed voice.

"Of course," replied Dorothy softly. "They are the Cloud Fairies."

"They seem like open-work," remarked the boy, gazing intently. "If I should squeeze one, there wouldn't be anything left of it."

In the open space between the clouds and the

black, bubbling sea far beneath, could be seen an occasional strange bird winging its way swiftly through the air. These birds were of enormous size, and reminded Zeb of the rocs he had read about in the Arabian Nights. They had fierce eyes and sharp talons and beaks, and the children hoped none of them would venture into the cavern.

"Well, I declare!" suddenly exclaimed the little Wizard. "What in the world is this?"

They turned around and found a man standing on the floor in the center of the cave, who bowed very politely when he saw he had attracted their attention. He was a very old man, bent nearly double; but the queerest thing about him was his white hair and beard. These were so long that they reached to his feet, and both the hair and the beard were carefully plaited into many braids, and the end of each braid fastened with a bow of colored ribbon.

"Where did you come from?" asked Dorothy wonderingly.

"No place at all," answered the man with the braids. "That is, not recently. Once I lived on top of the earth, but for many years I have had my factory in this spot—halfway up Pyramid Mountain."

"Are we only halfway up?" inquired the boy in a discouraged tone.

"I believe so, my lad," replied the braided man. "But as I have never been in either direction, down or up, since I arrived, I cannot be positive whether it is exactly halfway or not."

"Have you a factory in this place?" asked the Wizard, who had been examining the strange personage carefully.

"To be sure," said the other. "I am a great inventor, you must know, and I manufacture my products in this lonely spot."

"What are your products?" inquired the Wizard.

"Well, I make Assorted Flutters for flags and bunting, and a superior grade of Rustles for ladies' silk gowns."

"I thought so," said the Wizard with a sigh. "May we examine some of these articles?"

"Yes, indeed; come into my shop, please," and the braided man turned and led the way into a smaller cave where he evidently lived. Here, on a broad shelf, were several cardboard boxes of various sizes, each tied with cotton cord.

"This," said the man, taking up a box and handling it gently, "contains twelve dozen rustles—enough to last any lady a year. Will you buy it, my dear?" he asked, addressing Dorothy.

"My gown isn't silk," she said, smiling.

"Never mind. When you open the box the rustles will escape, whether you are wearing a silk dress or not," said the man seriously. Then he picked up another box. "In this," he continued, "are many assorted flutters. They are invaluable to make flags flutter on a still day, when there is no wind. You, sir," turning to the Wizard, "ought to have this assortment. Once you have tried my goods I am sure you will never be without them."

"I have no money with me," said the Wizard evasively.

"I do not want money," returned the braided man, "for I could not spend it in this deserted place if I had it. But I would like very much a blue hair-ribbon. You will notice my braids are tied with yellow, pink, brown, red, green, white and black; but I have no blue ribbons."

"I'll get you one!" cried Dorothy, who was sorry for the poor man; so she ran back to the buggy and took from her suitcase a pretty blue ribbon. It did her good to see how the braided man's eyes sparkled when he received this treasure.

"You have made me very, very happy, my dear!" he exclaimed; and then he insisted on the Wizard taking the box of flutters and the little girl accepting the box of rustles.

"You may need them, some time," he said, "and there is really no use in my manufacturing these things unless somebody uses them."

"Why did you leave the surface of the earth?" inquired the Wizard.

"I could not help it. It is a sad story, but if you will try to restrain your tears I will tell you about it. On earth I was a manufacturer of Imported Holes for American Swiss Cheese, and I will acknowledge that I supplied a superior article, which was in great demand. Also I made pores for porous plasters and high-grade holes for doughnuts and buttons. Finally I invented a new Adjustable Post Hole, which I thought would make my fortune. I manufactured a large quantity of these post holes, and having no room in which to store them I set them all end to end and put the top one in the ground. That made an extraordinary long hole, as you may imagine, and reached far down into the earth; and, as I leaned over it to try to see to the bottom, I lost my balance and tumbled in. Unfortunately, the hole led directly into the vast space you see outside this mountain; but I managed to catch a point of rock that projected from this cavern, and so saved myself from tumbling headlong into the black waves beneath, where the tongues of flame that dart out would certainly have consumed me. Here, then, I made my home; and although it is a lonely place I amuse myself making rustles and flutters, and so get along very nicely.''

When the braided man had completed this strange tale Dorothy nearly laughed, because it was all so absurd; but the Wizard tapped his forehead significantly, to indicate that he thought the poor man was crazy. So they politely bade him good day, and went back to the outer cavern to resume their journey.

Chapter 11

They Meet the Wooden Gargoyles

Another breathless climb brought our
adventurers to a third landing where there was a
rift in the mountain. On peering out all they
could see was rolling banks of clouds, so thick
that they obscured all else.

But the travelers were obliged to rest, and
while they were sitting on the rocky floor the
Wizard felt in his pocket and brought out the
nine tiny piglets. To his delight they were now
plainly visible, which proved that they had
passed beyond the influence of the magical
Valley of Voe.

"Why, we can see each other again!" cried
one joyfully.

"Yes," sighed Eureka, "and I also can see
you again, and the sight makes me dreadfully
hungry. Please, Mr. Wizard, may I eat just one
of the fat little piglets? You'd never miss *one* of
them, I'm sure!"

"What a horrid, savage beast!" exclaimed a piglet. "And after we've been such good friends, too, and played with one another!"

"When I'm not hungry, I love to play with you all," said the kitten demurely. "But when my stomach is empty it seems that nothing would fill it so nicely as a fat piglet."

"And we trusted you so!" said another of the nine reproachfully.

"And thought you were respectable!" said another.

"It seems we were mistaken," declared a third, looking at the kitten timorously. "No one with such murderous desires should belong to our party, I'm sure."

"You see, Eureka," remarked Dorothy, reprovingly, "you are making yourself disliked. There are certain things proper for a kitten to eat; but I never heard of a kitten eating a pig, under *any* cir'stances."

"Did you ever see such little pigs before?" asked the kitten. "They are no bigger than mice, and I'm sure mice are proper for me to eat."

"It isn't the bigness, dear; it's the variety," replied the girl. "These are Mr. Wizard's pets, just as you are my pet, and it wouldn't be any more proper for you to eat them than it would be for Jim to eat you."

"And that's just what I shall do if you don't let those little balls of pork alone," said Jim, glaring at the kitten with his round, big eyes. "If you injure any one of them I'll chew you up instantly."

The kitten looked at the horse thoughtfully, as if trying to decide whether he meant it or not.

"In that case," she said, "I'll leave them alone. You haven't many teeth left, Jim, but the few you have are sharp enough to make me shudder. So the piglets will be perfectly safe, hereafter, as far as I am concerned."

"That is right, Eureka," remarked the Wizard earnestly. "Let us all be a happy family and love one another."

Eureka yawned and stretched herself.

"I've always loved the piglets," she said, "but they don't love me."

"No one can love a person he's afraid of," asserted Dorothy. "If you behave, and don't scare the little pigs, I'm sure they'll grow very fond of you."

The Wizard now put the nine tiny ones back into his pocket and the journey was resumed.

"We must be pretty near the top now," said the boy, as they climbed wearily up the dark, winding stairway.

"The Country of the Gurgles can't be far from the top of the earth," remarked Dorothy. "It isn't very nice down here. I'd like to get home again, I'm sure."

No one replied to this, because they found they needed all their breath for the climb. The stairs had become narrower and Zeb and the Wizard often had to help Jim pull the buggy from one step to another, or keep it from jamming against the rocky walls.

At last, however, a dim light appeared ahead of them, which grew clearer and stronger as they advanced.

"Thank goodness we're nearly there!" panted the little Wizard.

Jim, who was in advance, saw the last stair before him and stuck his head above the rocky sides of the stairway. Then he halted, ducked down and began to back up, so that he nearly fell with the buggy onto the others.

"Let's go down again!" he said in his hoarse voice.

"Nonsense!" snapped the tired Wizard. "What's the matter with you, old man?"

"Everything," grumbled the horse. "I've taken a look at this place, and it's no fit country for real creatures to go to. Everything's dead up there —no flesh or blood or growing thing anywhere."

"Never mind; we can't turn back," said Dorothy. "And we don't intend to stay there, anyhow."

"It's dangerous," growled Jim in a stubborn tone.

"See here, my good steed," broke in the Wizard, "little Dorothy and I have been in many queer countries in our travels, and always escaped without harm. We've even been to the Marvelous Land of Oz—haven't we, Dorothy? —so we don't much care what the Country of Gargoyles is like. Go ahead, Jim, and whatever happens we'll make the best of it."

"All right," answered the horse. "This is your excursion and not mine; so if you get into trouble don't blame me."

With this speech he bent forward and dragged the buggy up the remaining steps. The others followed and soon they were all standing upon a broad platform and gazing at the most curious and startling sight their eyes had ever beheld.

"The Country of the Gargoyles is all wooden!" exclaimed Zeb; and so it was. The ground was sawdust and the pebbles scattered around were hard knots from trees, worn smooth in the course of time. There were odd wooden houses, with carved wooden flowers in the front yards. The tree trunks were of coarse wood, but the leaves of the trees were shavings. The patches of grass were splinters of wood, and where neither grass nor sawdust showed was a solid wooden flooring. Wooden birds fluttered among the trees and wooden cows were browsing upon the wooden grass; but the most amazing things of all were the wooden people— the creatures known as Gargoyles.

These were very numerous, for the place was thickly inhabited, and a large group of the queer people clustered near, gazing sharply upon the strangers who had emerged from the long spiral stairway.

The Gargoyles were very small of stature, being less than three feet in height. Their bodies were round, their legs short and thick and their arms extraordinarily long and stout. Their heads were too big for their bodies and their faces were decidedly ugly to look upon. Some had long, curved noses and chins, small eyes and wide, grinning mouths. Others had flat noses, protruding eyes, and ears that were shaped like those of an elephant. There were many types, indeed, scarcely two being alike; but all were equally disagreeable in appearance. The tops of their heads had no hair, but were carved into a variety of fantastic shapes, some having a row of points or balls around the top, other designs resembling flowers or vegetables, and still others have squares that looked like waffles cut criss-cross on their heads. They all wore short wooden wings which were fastened to their wooden bodies by means of wooden hinges with wooden screws, and with these wings they flew swiftly and noiselessly here and there, their legs being of little use to them.

This noiseless motion was one of the most peculiar things about the Gargoyles. They made no sounds at all, either in flying or trying to speak, and they conversed mainly by means of quick signals made with their wooden fingers or lips. Neither was there any sound to be heard anywhere throughout the wooden country. The birds did not sing, nor did the cows moo; yet there was more than ordinary activity everywhere.

The group of these queer creatures which was discovered clustered near the stairs at first remained staring and motionless, glaring with evil eyes at the intruders who had so suddenly appeared in their land. In turn the Wizard and the children, the horse and the kitten, examined the Gargoyles with the same silent attention.

"There's going to be trouble, I'm sure," remarked the horse. "Unhitch those tugs, Zeb, and set me free from the buggy, so I can fight comfortably."

"Jim's right," sighed the Wizard. "There's going to be trouble, and my sword isn't stout enough to cut up those wooden bodies—so I shall have to get out my revolvers."

He got his satchel from the buggy and, opening it, took out two deadly looking revolvers that made the children shrink back in alarm just to look at.

"What harm can the Gurgles do?" asked Dorothy. "They have no weapons to hurt us with."

"Each of their arms is a wooden club," answered the little man, "and I'm sure the creatures mean mischief, by the looks of their eyes. Even these revolvers can merely succeed in damaging a few of their wooden bodies, and after that we will be at their mercy."

"But why fight at all, in that case?" asked the girl.

"So I may die with a clear conscience," returned the Wizard, gravely. "It's every man's duty to do the best he knows how; and I'm going to do it."

"Wish I had an axe," said Zeb, who by now had unhitched the horse.

"If we had known we were coming we might have brought along several other useful things," responded the Wizard. "But we dropped into this adventure rather unexpectedly."

The Gargoyles had backed away a distance when they heard the sound of talking, for although our friends had spoken in low tones their words seemed loud in the silence surrounding them. But as soon as the conversation ceased the grinning, ugly creatures arose in a flock and flew swiftly toward the strangers, their long arms stretched out before them like the bowsprits of a fleet of sailboats. The horse had especially attracted their notice, because it was the biggest and strangest creature they had ever seen; so it became the center of their first attack.

But Jim was ready for them, and when he saw them coming he turned his heels toward them and began kicking out as hard as he could. Crack! crash! bang! went his iron-shod hoofs against the wooden bodies of the Gargoyles, and they were battered right and left with such force that they scattered like straws in the wind. But the noise and clatter seemed as dreadful to them as Jim's heels, for all who were able swiftly turned and flew away to a great distance. The others picked themselves up from the ground one by one and quickly rejoined their fellows, so for a moment the horse thought he had won the fight with ease.

But the Wizard was not so confident.

"Those wooden things are impossible to hurt," he said, "and all the damage Jim has done to them is to knock a few splinters from their noses and ears. That cannot make them look any uglier, I'm sure, and it is my opinion they will soon renew the attack."

"What made them fly away?" asked Dorothy.

"The noise, of course. Don't you remember how the Champion escaped them by shouting his battle cry?"

"Suppose we escape down the stairs, too," suggested the boy. "We have time, just now, and I'd rather face the invis'ble bears than those wooden imps."

"No," returned Dorothy stoutly, "it won't do to go back, for then we would never get home. Let's fight it out."

"That is what I advise," said the Wizard. "They haven't defeated us yet, and Jim is worth a whole army."

But the Gargoyles were clever enough not to attack the horse the next time. They advanced in a great swarm, having been joined by many more of their kind, and they flew straight over Jim's head to where the others were standing.

The Wizard raised one of his revolvers and fired into the throng of his enemies, and the shot resounded like a clap of thunder in that silent place.

Some of the wooden beings fell flat upon the ground, where they quivered and trembled in every limb; but most of them managed to wheel and escape again to a distance.

Zeb ran and picked up one of the Gargoyles that lay nearest to him. The top of its head was carved into a crown and the Wizard's bullet had struck it exactly in the left eye, which was a hard wooden knot. Half of the bullet stuck in the wood and half stuck out, so it had been the jar and the sudden noise that had knocked the creature down, more than the fact that it was really hurt. Before this crowned Gargoyle had recovered himself, Zeb had wound a strap several times aound its body, confining its wings and arms so that it could not move. Then, having tied the wooden creature securely, the boy buckled the strap and tossed his prisoner into the buggy. By that time the others had all retired.

Chapter 12

A Wonderful Escape

For a while the enemy hesitated to renew the attack. Then a few of them advanced until another shot from the Wizard's revolver made them retreat.

"That's fine," said Zeb. "We've got 'em on the run now, sure enough."

"But only for a time," replied the Wizard, shaking his head gloomily. "These revolvers are good for six shots each, but when those are gone we shall be helpless."

The Gargoyles seemed to realize this, for they sent a few of their band time after time to attack the strangers and draw the fire from the little man's revolvers. In this way none of them was shocked by the dreadful report more than once, for the main band kept far away and each time a new company was sent into the battle. When the Wizard had fired all of his twelve bullets, he had caused no damage to the enemy except to stun a few by the noise, and so he was no nearer to victory than in the beginning of the fray.

"What shall we do now?" asked Dorothy anxiously.

"Let's yell—all together," said Zeb.

"And fight at the same time," added the Wizard. "We will get near Jim, so that he can help us, and each one must take some weapon and do the best he can. I'll use my sword, although it isn't much account in this affair. Dorothy must take her parasol and open it suddenly when the wooden folks attack her. I haven't anything for you, Zeb."

"I'll use the king," said the boy, and pulled his prisoner out of the buggy. The bound Gargoyle's arms extended far out beyond its head, so by grasping its wrists Zeb found the king made a very good club. The boy was strong for one of his years, having always worked upon a farm; so he was likely to prove more dangerous to the enemy than the Wizard.

When the next company of Gargoyles advanced, our adventurers began yelling as if they had gone mad. Even the kitten gave a dreadfully shrill scream and at the same time Jim the cab-horse neighed loudly. This daunted the enemy for a time, but the defenders were soon out of breath. Perceiving this, as well as the fact that there were no more of the awful "bangs" to come from the revolvers, the Gargoyles advanced in a swarm as thick as bees, so that the air was filled with them.

Dorothy squatted upon the ground and put up her parasol, which nearly covered her and proved a great protection. The Wizard's sword blade snapped into a dozen pieces at the first blow he struck against the wooden people. Zeb pounded away with the Gargoyle he was using as a club until he had knocked down dozens of foes; but at the last they clustered so thickly about him that he no longer had room in which to swing his arms. The horse performed some wonderful kicking and even Eureka assisted when she leaped bodily upon the Gargoyles and scratched and bit at them like a wildcat.

But all this bravery amounted to nothing at all. The wooden things wound their long arms around Zeb and the Wizard and held them fast. Dorothy was captured in the same way, and numbers of the Gargoyles clung to Jim's legs, so weighting him down that the poor beast was helpless. Eureka made a desperate dash to escape and scampered along the ground like a streak; but a grinning Gargoyle flew after her and grabbed her before she had gone very far.

All of them expected nothing less than instant death; but to their surprise the wooden creatures flew into the air with them and bore them far away, over miles and miles of wooden country, until they came to a wooden city. The houses of this city had many corners, being square and six-sided and eight-sided. They were tower-like in shape and the best of them seemed old and weather-worn; yet all were strong and substantial.

To one of these houses which had neither doors nor windows, but only one broad opening far up underneath the roof, the prisoners were brought by their captors. The Gargoyles roughly pushed them into the opening, where there was a platform, and then flew away and left them. As they had no wings the strangers could not fly away, and if they jumped down from such a height they would surely be killed. The creatures had sense enough to reason that way, and the only mistake they made was in supposing the earth people were unable to overcome such ordinary difficulties.

Jim was brought with the others, although it took a good many Gargoyles to carry the big beast through the air and land him on the high platform, and the buggy was thrust in after him because it belonged to the party and the wooden folks had no idea what it was used for or whether it was alive or not. When Eureka's captor had thrown the kitten after the others the last Gargoyle silently disappeared, leaving our friends to breathe freely once more.

"What an awful fight!" said Dorothy, catching her breath in little gasps.

"Oh, I don't know," purred Eureka, smoothing her ruffled fur with her paw; "we didn't manage to hurt anybody, and nobody managed to hurt us."

"Thank goodness we are together again, even if we are prisoners," sighed the little girl.

"I wonder why they didn't kill us on the spot," remarked Zeb, who had lost his king in the struggle.

"They are probably keeping us for some ceremony," the Wizard answered reflectively. "But there is no doubt they intend to kill us as dead as possible in a short time."

"As dead as poss'ble would be pretty dead, wouldn't it?" asked Dorothy.

"Yes, my dear. But we have no need to worry about that just now. Let us examine our prison and see what it is like."

The space underneath the roof, where they stood, permitted them to see on all sides of the tall building, and they looked with much curiosity at the city spread out beneath them. Everything visible was made of wood, and the scene seemed stiff and extremely unnatural.

From their platform a stair descended into the house, and the children and the Wizard explored it after lighting a lantern to show them the way. Several stories of empty rooms rewarded their search, but nothing more; so after a time they came back to the platform again. Had there been any doors or windows in the lower rooms, or had not the boards of the house been so thick and stout, escape would have been easy; but to remain down below was like being in a cellar or the hold of a ship, and they did not like the darkness or the damp smell.

In this country, as in all others they had visited underneath the earth's surface, there was no night, a constant and strong light coming from some unknown source. Looking out, they could see into some of the houses near them, where there were open windows in abundance, and were able to mark the forms of the wooden Gargoyles moving about in their dwellings.

"This seems to be their time of rest," observed the Wizard. "All people need rest, even if they are made of wood, and as there is no night here they select a certain time of the day in which to sleep or doze.''

''I feel sleepy myself,'' remarked Zeb, yawning.

''Why, where's Eureka?'' cried Dorothy suddenly.

They all looked around, but the kitten was no place to be seen.

''She's gone out for a walk,'' said Jim gruffly.

''Where? On the roof?'' asked the girl.

''No; she just dug her claws into the wood and climbed down the sides of this house to the ground.''

''She couldn't climb *down*, Jim,'' said Dorothy. ''To climb means to go up.''

''Who said so?'' demanded the horse.

''My schoolteacher said so; and she knows a lot, Jim.''

''To 'climb down' is sometimes used as a figure of speech,'' remarked the Wizard.

''Well, this was a figure of a cat,'' said Jim, ''and she *went* down, anyhow, whether she climbed or crept.''

''Dear me! How careless Eureka is,'' exclaimed the girl, much distressed. ''The Gurgles will get her, sure!''

''Ha, ha!'' chuckled the old cab-horse. ''They're not 'Gurgles,' little maid; they're Gargoyles.''

''Never mind; they'll get Eureka, whatever they're called.''

''No they won't,'' said the voice of the kitten, and Eureka herself crawled over the edge of the platform and sat down quietly upon the floor.

"Wherever have you been, Eureka?" asked Dorothy sternly.

"Watching the wooden folks. They're too funny for anything, Dorothy. Just now they are all going to bed, and—what do you think?— they unhook the hinges of their wings and put them in a corner until they wake up again."

"What, the hinges?"

"No; the wings."

"That," said Zeb, "explains why this house is used by them for a prison. If any of the Gargoyles act badly, and have to be put in jail, they are brought here and their wings unhooked and taken away from them until they promise to be good."

The Wizard had listened intently to what Eureka had said.

"I wish we had some of those loose wings," he said.

"Could we fly with them?" asked Dorothy.

"I think so. If the Gargoyles can unhook the wings then the power to fly lies in the wings themselves, and not in the wooden bodies of the people who wear them. So, if we had the wings, we could probably fly as well as they do—at least while we are in their country and under the spell of its magic."

"But how would it help us to be able to fly?" questioned the girl.

"Come here," said the little man, and took her to one of the corners of the building. "Do you see that big rock standing on the hillside yonder?" he continued, pointing with his finger.

"Yes; it's a good way off, but I can see it," she replied.

"Well, inside that rock, which reaches up into the clouds, is an archway very much like the one we entered when we climbed the spiral stairway from the Valley of Voe. I'll get my spyglass, and then you can see it more plainly."

He fetched a small but powerful telescope, which had been in his satchel, and by its aid the little girl clearly saw the opening.

"Where does it lead to?" she asked.

"That I cannot tell," said the Wizard. "But we cannot now be far below the earth's surface, and that entrance may lead to another stairway that will bring us on top of our world again, where we belong. So, if we had the wings, and could escape the Gargoyles, we might fly to that rock and be saved."

"I'll get you the wings," said Zeb, who had thoughtfully listened to all this. "That is, if the kitten will show me where they are."

"But how can you get down?" inquired the girl wonderingly.

For answer Zeb began to unfasten Jim's harness, strap by strap, and to buckle one piece to another until he had made a long leather strip that would reach to the ground.

"I can climb down that, all right," he said.

"No you can't," remarked Jim, with a twinkle in his round eyes. "You may *go* down, but you can only *climb* up."

"Well, I'll climb up when I get back, then," said the boy with a laugh. "Now, Eureka, you'll have to show me the way to those wings."

"You must be very quiet," warned the kitten, "for if you make the least noise the Gargoyles will wake up. They can hear a pin drop."

"I'm not going to drop a pin," said Zeb.

He had fastened one end of the strap to a wheel of the buggy, and now he let the line dangle over the side of the house.

"Be careful," cautioned Dorothy earnestly.

"I will," said the boy, and let himself slide over the edge.

The girl and the Wizard leaned over and watched Zeb work his way carefully downward, hand over hand, until he stood upon the ground below. Eureka clung with her claws to the wooden side of the house and let herself down easily. Then together they crept away to enter the low doorway of a neighboring dwelling.

The watchers waited in breathless suspense until the boy again appeared, his arms now full of the wooden wings.

When he came to where the strap was hanging he tied the wings all in a bunch to the end of the line, and the Wizard drew them up. Then the line was let down again for Zeb to climb up by. Eureka quickly followed him, and soon they were all standing together upon the platform, with eight of the much prized wooden wings beside them.

The boy was no longer sleepy, but full of energy and excitement. He put the harness together again and hitched Jim to the buggy. Then, with the Wizard's help, he tried to fasten some of the wings to the old cab-horse.

This was no easy task, because half of each one of the hinges of the wings was missing, it being still fastened to the body of the Gargoyle who had used it. However, the Wizard went once more to his satchel—which seemed to contain a surprising variety of odds and ends—and brought out a spool of strong wire, by means of which they managed to fasten four of the wings to Jim's harness, two near his head and two near his tail. They were a bit wiggly, but secure enough if only the harness held together.

The other four wings were then fastened to the buggy, two on each side, for the buggy must bear the weight of the children and the Wizard as it flew through the air.

These preparations had not consumed a great deal of time, but the sleeping Gargoyles were beginning to wake up and move around, and soon some of them would be hunting for their missing wings. So the prisoners resolved to leave their prison at once.

They mounted into the buggy, Dorothy holding Eureka safe in her lap. The girl sat in the middle of the seat, with Zeb and the Wizard on each side of her. When all was ready the boy shook the reins and said:

"Fly away, Jim!"

"Which wings must I flop first?" asked the cab-horse undecidedly.

"Flop them all together," suggested the Wizard.

"Some of them are crooked," objected the horse.

"Never mind; we will steer with the wings on the buggy," said Zeb. "Just you light out and make for that rock, Jim; and don't waste any time about it, either."

So the horse gave a groan, flopped its four wings all together, and flew away from the platform. Dorothy was a little anxious about the success of their trip, for the way Jim arched his long neck and spread out his bony legs as he fluttered and floundered through the air was enough to make anybody nervous. He groaned, too, as if frightened, and the wings creaked dreadfully because the Wizard had forgotten to oil them; but they kept fairly good time with the wings of the buggy, so that they made excellent progress from the start. The only thing that anyone could complain of with justice was the fact that they wobbled first up and then down, as if the road were rocky instead of being as smooth as the air could make it.

The main point, however, was that they flew, and flew swiftly, if a bit unevenly, toward the rock for which they had headed.

Some of the Gargoyles saw them, presently, and lost no time in collecting a band to pursue the escaping prisoners; so that when Dorothy happened to look back she saw them coming in a great cloud that almost darkened the sky.

Chapter 13

The Den of the Dragonettes

Our friends had a good start and were able to maintain it, for with their eight wings they could go just as fast as could the Gargoyles. All the way to the great rock the wooden people followed them, and when Jim finally alighted at the mouth of the cavern the pursuers were still some distance away.

"But, I'm afraid they'll catch us yet," said Dorothy, greatly excited.

"No; we must stop them," declared the Wizard. "Quick Zeb, help me pull off these wooden wings!"

They tore off the wings, for which they had no further use, and the Wizard piled them in a heap just outside the entrance to the cavern. Then he poured over them all the kerosene oil that was left in his oilcan, and lighting a match set fire to the pile.

The flames leaped up at once and the bonfire

began to smoke and roar and crackle just as the great army of wooden Gargoyles arrived. The creatures drew back at once, being filled with fear and horror; for such a dreadful thing as a fire they had never before known in all the history of their wooden land.

Inside the archway were several doors, leading to different rooms built into the mountain, and Zeb and the Wizard lifted these wooden doors from their hinges and tossed them all on the flames.

"That will prove a barrier for some time to come," said the little man, smiling pleasantly all over his wrinkled face at the success of their stratagem. "Perhaps the flames will set fire to all that miserable wooden country, and if it does the loss will be very small and the Gargoyles never will be missed. But come, my children; let us explore the mountain and discover which way we must go in order to escape from this cavern, which is getting to be almost as hot as a bake-oven."

To their disappointment there was within this mountain no regular flight of steps by means of which they could mount to the earth's surface. A sort of inclined tunnel led upward for a way, and they found the floor of it both rough and steep. Then a sudden turn brought them to a narrow gallery where the buggy could not pass. This delayed and bothered them for a while, because they did not wish to leave the buggy behind them. It carried their baggage and was useful to ride in wherever there were good roads, and since it had accompanied them so far in their travels they felt it their duty to preserve it. So Zeb and the Wizard set to work and took off the wheels and the top, and then they put the buggy edgewise, so it would take up the smallest space. In this position they managed, with the aid of the patient cab-horse, to drag the vehicle through the narrow part of the passage. It was not a great distance, fortunately, and when the path grew broader they put the buggy together again and proceeded more comfortably. But the road was nothing more than a series of rifts or cracks in the mountain, and it went zigzag in every direction, slanting first up and then down until they were puzzled as to whether they were any nearer to the top of the earth than when they had started, hours before.

"Anyhow," said Dorothy, "we've 'scaped those awful Gurgles, and that's *one* comfort!"

"Probably the Gargoyles are still busy trying to put out the fire," returned the Wizard. "But even if they succeeded in doing that it would be very difficult for them to fly amongst these rocks; so I am sure we need fear them no longer."

Once in a while they would come to a deep crack in the floor, which made the way quite dangerous; but there was still enough oil in the lanterns to give them light, and the cracks were not so wide but that they were able to jump over them. Sometimes they had to climb over heaps of loose rock, where Jim could scarcely drag the buggy. At such times Dorothy, Zeb and the Wizard all pushed behind, and lifted the wheels over the roughest places; so they managed, by dint of hard work, to keep going. But the little party was both weary and discouraged when at last, on turning a sharp corner, the wanderers found themselves in a vast cave arching high over their heads and having a smooth, level floor.

The cave was circular in shape, and all around its edge, near to the ground, appeared groups of dull yellow lights, two of them being always side by side. These were motionless at first, but soon began to flicker more brightly and to sway slowly from side to side and then up and down.

"What sort of a place is this?" asked the boy, trying to see more clearly through the gloom.

"I cannot imagine, I'm sure," answered the Wizard, also peering about.

"Woogh!" snarled Eureka, arching her back until her hair stood straight on end. "It's a den of alligators, or crocodiles, or some other dreadful creatures! Don't you see their terrible eyes?"

"Eureka sees better in the dark than we can," whispered Dorothy. "Tell us, dear, what do the creatures look like?" she asked, addressing her pet.

"I simply can't describe 'em," answered the kitten, shuddering. "Their eyes are like pie plates and their mouths like coal scuttles. But their bodies don't seem very big."

"Where are they?" inquired the girl.

"They are in little pockets all around the edge of this cavern. Oh, Dorothy—you can't imagine what horrid things they are! They're uglier than the Gargoyles."

"Tut-tut! Be careful how you criticize your neighbors," spoke a rasping voice nearby. "As a matter of fact you are rather ugly-looking creatures yourselves, and I'm sure mother has often told us we were the loveliest and prettiest things in all the world."

Hearing these words our friends turned in the direction of the sound, and the Wizard held his lanterns so that their light would flood one of the little pockets in the rock.

"Why, it's a dragon!" he exclaimed.

"No," answered the owner of the big yellow eyes which were blinking at them so steadily, "you are wrong about that. We hope to grow to be dragons someday, but just now we're only dragonettes."

"What's that?" asked Dorothy, gazing fearfully at the great scaly head, the yawning mouth and the big eyes.

"Young dragons, of course; but we are not allowed to call ourselves real dragons until we get our full growth," was the reply. "The big dragons are very proud, and don't think children amount to much; but mother says that someday we will all be very powerful and important."

"Where is your mother?" asked the Wizard, anxiously looking around.

"She has gone up to the top of the earth to hunt for our dinner. If she has good luck she will bring us an elephant, or a brace of rhinoceroses, or perhaps a few dozen people to stay our hunger."

"Oh; are you hungry?" inquired Dorothy, drawing back.

"Very," said the dragonette, snapping its jaws.

"And—and—do you eat people?"

"To be sure, when we can get them. But they've been very scarce for a few years and we usually have to be content with elephants or buffaloes," answered the creature in a regretful tone.

"How old are you?" inquired Zeb, who stared at the yellow eyes as if fascinated.

"Quite young, I grieve to say; and all of my brothers and sisters that you see here are practically my own age. If I remember rightly, we were sixty-six years old the day before yesterday."

"But that isn't young!" cried Dorothy in amazement.

"No?" drawled the dragonette. "It seems to me very babyish."

"How old is your mother?" asked the girl.

"Mother's about two thousand years old; but she carelessly lost track of her age a few centuries ago and skipped several hundreds. She's a little fussy, you know, and afraid of growing old, being a widow and still in her prime."

"I should think she would be," agreed Dorothy. Then, after a moment's thought, she asked: "Are we friends or enemies? I mean, will you be good to us, or do you intend to eat us?"

"As for that, we dragonettes would love to eat you, my child; but unfortunately mother has tied all our tails around the rocks at the back of our individual caves, so that we cannot crawl out to get you. If you choose to come nearer we will make a mouthful of you in a wink; but unless you do you will remain quite safe."

There was a regretful accent in the creature's voice, and at the words all the other dragonettes sighed dismally.

Dorothy felt relieved. Presently she asked:

"Why did your mother tie your tails?"

"Oh, she is sometimes gone for several weeks on her hunting trips, and if we were not tied we would crawl all over the mountain and fight with each other and get into a lot of mischief. Mother usually knows what she is about, but she made a mistake this time; for you are sure to escape us unless you come too near, and you probably won't do that."

"No, indeed!" said the little girl. "We don't wish to be eaten by such awful beasts."

"Permit me to say," returned the dragonette, "that you are rather impolite to call us names, knowing that we cannot resent your insults. We consider ourselves very beautiful in appearance, for mother has told us so, and she knows. And we are of an excellent family and have a pedigree that I challenge any humans to equal, as it extends back about twenty thousand years, to the time of the famous Green Dragon of Atlantis, who lived in a time when humans had not yet been created. Can you match that pedigree, little girl?"

"Well," said Dorothy, "I was born on a farm in Kansas, and I guess that's being just as 'spectable and haughty as living in a cave with your tail tied to a rock. If it isn't I'll have to stand it, that's all."

"Tastes differ," murmured the dragonette, slowly drooping its scaly eyelids over its yellow eyes, until they looked like half-moons.

Being reassured by the fact that the creatures could not crawl out of their rock pockets, the children and the Wizard now took time to examine them more closely. The heads of the dragonettes were as big as barrels and covered with hard, greenish scales that glittered brightly under the light of the lanterns. Their front legs, which grew just back of their heads, were also strong and big; but their bodies were smaller around than their heads, and dwindled away in a long line until their tails were slim as a shoe-string. Dorothy thought, if it had taken them sixty-six years to grow to this size, that it would be fully a hundred years more before they could hope to call themselves dragons, and that seemed like a good while to wait to grow up.

"It occurs to me," said the Wizard, "that we ought to get out of this place before the mother dragon comes back."

"Don't hurry," called one of the dragon-ettes. "Mother will be glad to meet you, I'm sure."

"You may be right," replied the Wizard, "but we're a little particular about associating with strangers. Will you kindly tell us which way your mother went to get on top the earth?"

"That is not a fair question to ask us," declared another dragonette. "For, if we told you truly, you might escape us altogether; and if we told you an untruth we would be naughty and deserve to be punished."

"Then," decided Dorothy, "we must find our way out the best we can."

They circled all around the cavern, keeping a good distance away from the blinking yellow eyes of the dragonettes, and presently discovered that there were two paths leading from the wall opposite to the place where they had entered. They selected one of these at a venture and hurried along it as fast as they could go, for they had no idea when the mother dragon would be back and were very anxious not to make her acquaintance.

Chapter 14
Ozma Uses the Magic Belt

For a considerable distance the way led straight upward in a gentle incline, and the wanderers made
such good progress that they grew hopeful and
eager, thinking they might see sunshine at any
minute. But at length they came unexpectedly
upon a huge rock that shut off the passage and
blocked them from proceeding a single step farther.

This rock was separate from the rest of the
mountain and was in motion, turning slowly
around and around as if upon a pivot. When first
they came to it there was a solid wall before them;
but presently it revolved until there was exposed a
wide, smooth path across it to the other side. This
appeared so unexpectedly that they were unpre-
pared to take advantage of it at first, and allowed
the rocky wall to swing around again before they
had decided to pass over. But they knew now that
there was a means of escape and so waited patiently
until the path appeared for the second time.

The children and the Wizard rushed across the moving rock and sprang into the passage beyond, landing safely though a little out of breath. Jim the cab-horse came last, and the rocky wall almost caught him; for just as he leaped to the floor of the further passage the wall swung across it and a loose stone that the buggy wheels knocked against fell into the narrow crack where the rock turned, and became wedged there.

They heard a crunching, grinding sound, a loud snap, and the turntable came to a stop with its broadest surface shutting off the path from which they had come.

"Never mind," said Zeb, "we don't want to get back anyhow."

"I'm not so sure of that," returned Dorothy. "The mother dragon may come down and catch us here."

"It is possible," agreed the Wizard, "if this proves to be the path she usually takes. But I have been examining this tunnel, and I do not see any signs of so large a beast having passed through it."

"Then we're all right," said the girl, "for if the dragon went the other way she can't poss'bly get to us now."

"Of course not, my dear. But there is another thing to consider. The mother dragon probably knows the road to the earth's surface, and if she went the other way then we have come the wrong way," said the Wizard thoughtfully.

"Dear me!" cried Dorothy. "That would be unlucky, wouldn't it?"

"Very. Unless this passage also leads to the top of the earth," said Zeb. "For my part, if we manage to get out of here I'll be glad it isn't the way the dragon goes."

"So will I," returned Dorothy. "It's enough to have your pedigree flung in your face by those saucy dragonettes. No one knows what the mother might do."

They now moved on again, creeping slowly up another steep incline. The lanterns were beginning to grow dim, and the Wizard poured the remaining oil from one into the other, so that the one light would last longer. But their journey was almost over, for in a short time they reached a small cave from which there was no further outlet.

They did not realize their ill fortune at first, for their hearts were gladdened by the sight of a ray of sunshine coming through a small crack in the roof of the cave, far overhead. That meant that their world —the real world—was not very far away, and that the succession of perilous adventures they had encountered had at last brought them near the earth's surface, which meant home to them. But when the adventurers looked more carefully around them they discovered that they were in a strong prison from which there was no hope of escape.

"But we're *almost* on earth again," cried Dorothy, "for there is the sun—the most *beau'ful* sun that shines!" and she pointed eagerly at the crack in the distant roof.

"Almost on earth isn't being there," said the kitten in a discontented tone. "It wouldn't be possible for even me to get up to that crack—or through it if I got there."

"It appears that the path ends here," announced the Wizard gloomily.

"And there is no way to go back," added Zeb, with a low whistle of perplexity.

"I was sure it would come to this, in the end," remarked the old cab-horse. "Folks don't fall into the middle of the earth and then get back again to tell of their adventures—not in real life. And the whole thing has been unnatural because that cat and I are both able to talk your language, and to understand the words you say."

"And so can the nine tiny piglets," added Eureka. "Don't forget them, for I may have to eat them, after all."

"I've heard animals talk before," said Dorothy, "and no harm came of it."

"Were you ever before shut up in a cave, far under the earth, with no way of getting out?" inquired the horse seriously.

"No," answered Dorothy. "But don't you lose heart, Jim, for I'm sure this isn't the end of our story, by any means."

The reference to the piglets reminded the Wizard that his pets had not enjoyed much exercise lately, and must be tired of their prison in his pocket. So he sat down upon the floor of the cave, brought the piglets out one by one, and allowed them to run around as much as they pleased.

"My dears," he said to them, "I'm afraid I've got you into a lot of trouble, and that you will never again be able to leave this gloomy cave."

"What's wrong?" asked a piglet. "We've been in the dark quite a while, and you may as well explain what has happened."

The Wizard told them of the misfortune that had overtaken the wanderers.

"Well," said another piglet, "you are a wizard, are you not?"

"I am," replied the little man.

"Then you can do a few wizzes and get us out of this hole," declared the tiny one, with much confidence.

"I could if I happened to be a real wizard," returned the master sadly. "But I'm not, my piggy-wees; I'm a humbug wizard."

"Nonsense!" cried several of the piglets together.

"You can ask Dorothy," said the little man in an injured tone.

"It's true enough," returned the girl earnestly. "Our friend Oz is merely a humbug wizard, for he once proved it to me. He can do several very wonderful things—if he knows how. But he can't wiz a single thing if he hasn't the tools and machinery to work with."

"Thank you, my dear, for doing me justice," responded the Wizard gratefully. "To be accused of being a real wizard, when I'm not, is a slander I will not tamely submit to. But I am one of the greatest humbug wizards that ever lived, and you will realize this when we have all starved together and our bones are scattered over the floor of this lonely cave."

"I don't believe we'll realize anything, when it comes to that," remarked Dorothy, who had been deep in thought. "But I'm not going to scatter my bones just yet, because I need them, and you prob'ly need yours, too."

"We are helpless to escape," sighed the Wizard.

"*We* may be helpless," answered Dorothy, smiling at him, "but there are others who can do more than we can. Cheer up, friends, I'm sure Ozma will help us."

"Ozma!" exclaimed the Wizard. "Who is Ozma?"

"The girl that rules the marvelous Land of Oz," was the reply. "She's a friend of mine, for I met her in the Land of Ev, not long ago, and went to Oz with her."

"For the second time?" asked the Wizard, with great interest.

"Yes. The first time I went to Oz I found you there, ruling the Emerald City. After you went up in a balloon, and escaped us, I got back to Kansas by means of a pair of magical silver shoes."

"I remember those shoes," said the little man nodding. "They once belonged to the Wicked Witch. Have you them here with you?"

"No; I lost them somewhere in the air," explained the child. "But the second time I went to the Land of Oz I owned the Nome King's Magic Belt, which is much more powerful than were the Silver Shoes."

"Where is that Magic Belt?" inquired the Wizard, who had listened with great interest.

"Ozma has it; for its powers won't work in a common, ordinary country like the United States. Anyone in a fairy country like the Land of Oz can do anything with it; so I left it with my friend the Princess Ozma, who used it to wish me in Australia with Uncle Henry.''

''And were you?'' asked Zeb, astonished at what he heard.

''Of course; in just a jiffy. And Ozma has an enchanted picture hanging in her room that shows her the exact scene where any of her friends may be, at any time she chooses. All she has to do is to say: 'I wonder what So-and-so is doing,' and at once the picture shows where her friend is and what the friend is doing. That's *real* magic, Mr. Wizard; isn't it? Well, every day at four o'clock Ozma has promised to look at me in that picture, and if I am in need of help I am to make her a certain sign and she will put on the Nome King's Magic Belt and wish me to be with her in Oz.''

''Do you mean that Princess Ozma will see this cave in her enchanted picture, and see all of us here, and what we are doing?'' demanded Zeb.

''Of course; when it is four o'clock,'' she replied, with a laugh at his startled expression.

''And when you make a sign she will bring you to her in the Land of Oz?'' continued the boy.

''That's it, exactly; by means of the Magic Belt.''

''Then,'' said the Wizard, ''you will be saved, little Dorothy; and I am very glad of it. The rest of us will die much more cheerfully when we know you have escaped our sad fate.''

''*I* won't die cheerfully!'' protested the kitten.

"There's nothing cheerful about dying that I could ever see, although they say a cat has nine lives, and so must die nine times."

"Have you ever died yet?" inquired the boy.

"No, and I'm not anxious to begin," said Eureka.

"Don't worry, dear," Dorothy exclaimed, "I'll hold you in my arms, and take you with me."

"Take us, too!" cried the nine tiny piglets, all in one breath.

"Perhaps I can," answered Dorothy. "I'll try."

"Couldn't you manage to hold me in your arms?" asked the cab-horse.

Dorothy laughed.

"I'll do better than that," she promised, "for I can easily save you all, once I am myself in the Land of Oz."

"How?" they asked.

"By using the Magic Belt. All I need do is to wish you with me, and there you'll be—safe in the royal palace!"

"Good!" cried Zeb.

"I built that palace, and the Emerald City, too," remarked the Wizard in a thoughtful tone, "and I'd like to see them again, for I was very happy among the Munchkins and Winkies and Quadlings and Gillikins."

"Who are they?" asked the boy.

"The four nations that inhabit the Land of Oz," was the reply. "I wonder if they would treat me nicely if I went there again."

"Of course they would!" declared Dorothy. "They are still proud of their former Wizard, and often speak of you kindly."

"Do you happen to know whatever became of the Tin Woodman and the Scarecrow?" he inquired.

"They live in Oz yet," said the girl, "and are very important people."

"And the Cowardly Lion?"

"Oh, he lives there too, with his friend the Hungry Tiger; and Billina is there, because she liked the place better than Kansas, and wouldn't go with me to Australia."

"I'm afraid I don't know the Hungry Tiger and Billina," said the Wizard, shaking his head. "Is Billina a girl?"

"No; she's a yellow hen, and a great friend of mine. You're sure to like Billina, when you know her," asserted Dorothy.

"Your friends sound like a menagerie," remarked Zeb uneasily. "Couldn't you wish me in some safer place than Oz?"

"Don't worry," replied the girl. "You'll just love the folks in Oz, when you get acquainted. What time is it, Mr. Wizard?"

The little man looked at his watch—a big silver one that he carried in his vest pocket.

"Half-past three," he said.

"Then we must wait for half an hour," she continued; "but it won't take long, after that, to carry us all to the Emerald City."

They sat silently thinking for a time. Then Jim suddenly asked:

"Are there any horses in Oz?"

"Only one," replied Dorothy, "and he's a saw-horse."

"A what?"

123

"A sawhorse. Princess Ozma once brought him to life with a witch powder, when she was a boy."

"Was Ozma once a boy?" asked Zeb wonderingly.

"Yes; a wicked witch enchanted her, so she could not rule her kingdom. But she's a girl now, and the sweetest, loveliest girl in all the world."

"A sawhorse is a thing they saw boards on," remarked Jim, with a sniff.

"It is when it's not alive," acknowledged the girl. "But this sawhorse can trot as fast as you can, Jim; and he's very wise, too."

"Pah! I'll race the miserable wooden donkey any day in the week!" cried the cab-horse.

Dorothy did not reply to that. She felt that Jim would know more about the Sawhorse later on.

The time dragged wearily enough to the eager watchers, but finally the Wizard announced that four o'clock had arrived, and Dorothy caught up the kitten and began to make the signal that had been agreed upon to the faraway, invisible Ozma.

"Nothing seems to happen," said Zeb doubtfully.

"Oh, we must give Ozma time to put on the Magic Belt," replied the girl.

She had scarcely spoken the words when she suddenly disappeared from the cave, and with her went the kitten. There had been no sound of any kind and no warning. One moment Dorothy sat beside them with the kitten in her lap, and a moment later the horse, the piglets, the Wizard and the boy were all that remained in the underground prison.

"I believe we will soon follow her," announced the Wizard, in a tone of great relief; "for I know something about the magic of the fairyland that is called the Land of Oz. Let us be ready, for we may be sent for any minute."

He put the piglets safely away in his pocket again and then he and Zeb got into the buggy and sat expectantly upon the seat.

"Will it hurt?" asked the boy, in a voice that trembled a little.

"Not at all," replied the Wizard. "It will all happen as quick as a wink."

And that was the way it did happen.

The cab-horse gave a nervous start and Zeb began to rub his eyes to make sure he was not asleep. For they were in the streets of a beautiful emerald-green city, bathed in a grateful green light that was especially pleasing to their eyes, and surrounded by merry-faced people in gorgeous green-and-gold costumes of many extraordinary designs.

Before them were the jewel-studded gates of a magnificent palace, and now the gates opened slowly as if inviting them to enter the courtyard, where splendid flowers were blooming and pretty fountains shot their silvery sprays into the air.

Zeb shook the reins to rouse the cab-horse from his stupor of amazement, for the people were beginning to gather around and stare at the strangers.

"Gid-dap!" cried the boy, and at the word Jim slowly trotted into the courtyard and drew the buggy along the jewelled driveway to the great entrance of the royal palace.

Chapter 15
Old Friends Are Reunited

Many servants dressed in handsome uniforms stood ready to welcome the new arrivals, and when the Wizard got out of the buggy a pretty girl in a green gown cried out in surprise:

"Why, it's Oz, the Wonderful Wizard, come back again!"

The little man looked at her closely and then took both the maiden's hands in his and shook them cordially.

"On my word," he exclaimed, "it's little Jellia Jamb—as pert and pretty as ever!"

"Why not, Mr. Wizard?" asked Jellia, bowing low. "But I'm afraid you cannot rule the Emerald City, as you used to, because we now have a beautiful Princess whom everyone loves dearly."

And the people will not willingly part with her," added a tall soldier in a Captain-General's uniform.

The Wizard turned to look at him.

"Did you not wear green whiskers at one time?" he asked.

"Yes," said the soldier; "but I shaved them off long ago, and since then I have risen from a private to be the Chief General of the Royal Armies."

"That's nice," said the little man. "But I assure you, my good people, that I do not wish to rule the Emerald City," he added earnestly.

"In that case you are very welcome!" cried all the servants, and it pleased the Wizard to note the respect with which the royal retainers bowed before him. His fame had not been forgotten in the Land of Oz, by any means.

"Where is Dorothy?" inquired Zeb anxiously, as he left the buggy and stood beside his friend the little Wizard.

"She is with the Princess Ozma, in the private rooms of the palace," replied Jellia Jamb. "But she has ordered me to make you welcome and to show you to your apartments."

The boy looked around him with wondering eyes. Such magnificence and wealth as was displayed in this palace was more than he had ever dreamed of, and he could scarcely believe that all the gorgeous glitter was real and not tinsel.

"What's to become of me?" asked the horse uneasily. He had been considerable of life in the cities in his younger days, and knew that this regal palace was no place for him.

It perplexed even Jellia Jamb for a time, to know what to do with the animal. The green maiden was much astonished at the sight of so unusual a creature, for horses were unknown in this Land; but those who lived in the Emerald City were apt to be astonished by queer sights, so after inspecting the cab-horse and noting the mild look in his big eyes the girl decided not to be afraid of him.

"There are no stables here," said the Wizard, "unless some have been built since I went away."

"We have never needed them before," answered Jellia; "for the Sawhorse lives in a room of the palace, being much smaller and more natural in appearance than this great beast you have brought with you."

"Do you mean that I'm a freak?" asked Jim angrily.

"Oh, no," she hastened to say, "there may be many more like you in the place you came from, but in Oz any horse but a Sawhorse is unusual."

This mollified Jim a little, and after some thought the green maiden decided to give the cab-horse a room in the palace, such a big building having many rooms that were seldom in use.

So Zeb unharnessed Jim, and several of the servants then led the horse around to the rear, where they selected a nice large apartment that he could have all to himself.

Then Jellia said to the Wizard:

"Your own room—which was back of the great Throne Room—has been vacant ever since you left us. Would you like it again?"

"Yes, indeed!" returned the little man. "It will seem like being at home again, for I lived in that room for many, many years."

He knew the way to it, and a servant followed him, carrying his satchel. Zeb was also escorted to a room—so grand and beautiful that he almost feared to sit in the chairs or lie upon the bed, lest he might dim their splendor. In the closets he discovered many fancy costumes of rich velvets and brocades, and one of the attendants told him to dress himself in any of the clothes that pleased him and to be prepared to dine with the Princess and Dorothy in an hour's time.

Opening from the chamber was a fine bathroom having a marble tub with perfumed water; so the boy, still dazed by the novelty of his surroundings, indulged in a good bath and then selected a maroon velvet costume with silver buttons to replace his own soiled and much-worn clothing. There were silk stockings and soft leather slippers with diamond buckles to accompany his new costume, and when he was fully dressed Zeb looked much more dignified and imposing than ever before in his life.

He was all ready when an attendant came to escort him to the presence of the Princess; he followed bashfully and was ushered into a room more dainty and attractive than it was splendid. Here he found Dorothy seated beside a young girl so marvelously beautiful that the boy stopped suddenly with a gasp of admiration.

But Dorothy sprang up and ran to seize her friend's hand, drawing him impulsively toward the lovely Princess, who smiled most graciously upon her guest. Then the Wizard entered, and his presence relieved the boy's embarrassment. The little man was clothed in black velvet, with many sparkling emerald ornaments decorating his breast; but his bald head and wrinkled features made him appear more amusing than impressive.

Ozma had been quite curious to meet the famous man who had built the Emerald City and united the Munchkins, Gillikins, Quadlings, and Winkies into one people; so when they were all four seated at the dinner table the Princess said:

"Please tell me, Mr. Wizard, whether you called yourself Oz after this great country, or whether you believe my country is called Oz after you. It is a matter that I have long wished to inquire about, because you are of a strange race and my own name is Ozma. No one, I am sure, is better able to explain this mystery than you."

"That is true," answered the little Wizard. "Therefore it will give me pleasure to explain my connection with your country. In the first place, I must tell you that I was born in Omaha, and my father, who was a politician, named me Oscar Zoroaster Phadrig Isaac Norman Henkle Emmannuel Ambroise Diggs, Diggs being the last name because he could think of no more to go before it. Taken altogether, it was a dreadfully long name to weigh down a poor innocent child, and one of the hardest lessons I ever learned was to remember my own name. When I grew up I just called myself O. Z., because the other initials were P-I-N-H-E-A-D; and that spelled 'pinhead,' which was a reflection on my intelligence."

"Surely no one could blame you for cutting your name short," said Ozma sympathetically. "But didn't you cut it almost too short?"

"Perhaps so," replied the Wizard. "When a young man, I ran away from home and joined a circus. I used to call myself a Wizard, and do tricks of ventriloquism."

"What does that mean?" asked the Princess.

"Throwing my voice into any object I pleased, to make it appear that the object was speaking instead of me. Also I began to make balloon ascensions. On my balloon and on all the other articles I used in the circus I painted the two initials: 'O. Z.,' to show that those things belonged to me.

"One day my balloon ran away with me and brought me across the deserts to this beautiful country. When the people saw me come from the sky they naturally thought me some superior creature, and bowed down before me. I told them I was a Wizard, and showed them some easy tricks that amazed them; and when they saw the initials painted on the balloon they called me Oz."

"Now I begin to understand," said the Princess, smiling.

"At that time," continued the Wizard, busily eating his soup while talking, "there were four separate countries in this Land, each one of the four being ruled by a Witch. But the people thought my power was greater than that of the Witches; and perhaps the Witches thought so too, for they never dared oppose me. I ordered the Emerald City to be built just where the four countries cornered together, and when it was completed I announced myself the Ruler of the Land of Oz, which included all the four countries of the Munchkins, the Gillikins, the Winkies, and the Quadlings. Over this Land I ruled in peace for many years, until I grew old and longed to see my native city once again. So when Dorothy was first blown to this place by a cyclone I arranged to go away with her in a balloon; but the balloon escaped too soon and carried me back alone. After many adventures I reached Omaha, only to find that all my old friends were dead or had moved away. So, having nothing else to do, I joined a circus again, and made my balloon ascensions until the earthquake caught me.''

"That is quite a history," said Ozma; "but there is a little more history about the Land of Oz that you do not seem to understand—perhaps for the reason that no one ever told it you. Many years before you came here this Land was united under one Ruler, as it is now, and the Ruler's name was always 'Oz,' which means in our language 'Great and Good'; or, if the Ruler happened to be a woman, her name was always 'Ozma.' But once upon a time four Witches leagued together to depose the king and rule the four parts of the kingdom themselves; so when the Ruler, my grandfather, was hunting one day, one Wicked Witch named Mombi stole him and carried him away, keeping him a close prisoner. Then the Witches divided up the kingdom, and ruled the four parts of it until you came here. That was why the people were so glad to see you, and why they thought from your initials that you were their rightful ruler.''

"But, at that time," said the Wizard thought-fully, "there were two Good Witches and two Wicked Witches ruling in the land."

"Yes," replied Ozma, "because a good Witch had conquered Mombi in the North and Glinda the Good had conquered the evil Witch in the South. But Mombi was still my grand-father's jailor, and afterward my father's jailor. When I was born she transformed me into a boy, hoping that no one would ever recognize me and know that I was the rightful Princess of the Land of Oz. But I escaped from her and am now the Ruler of my people."

"I am very glad of that," said the Wizard, "and hope you will consider me one of your most faithful and devoted subjects."

"We owe a great deal to the Wonderful Wizard," continued the Princess, "for it was you who built this splendid Emerald City."

"Your people built it," he answered. "I only bossed the job, as we say in Omaha."

"But you ruled it wisely and well for many years," said she, "and made the people proud of your magical art. So, as you are now too old to wander abroad and work in a circus, I offer you a home here as long as you live. You shall be the Official Wizard of my kingdom, and be treated with every respect and consideration."

"I accept your kind offer with gratitude, gracious Princess," the little man said in a soft voice, and they could all see that teardrops were standing in his keen old eyes. It meant a good deal to him to secure a home like this.

"He's only a humbug Wizard though," said Dorothy, smiling at him.

"And that is the safest kind of a Wizard to have," replied Ozma promptly.

"Oz can do some good tricks, humbug or no humbug," announced Zeb, who was now feeling more at ease.

"He shall amuse us with his tricks tomorrow," said the Princess. "I have sent messengers to summon all of Dorothy's old friends to meet her and give her welcome, and they ought to arrive very soon now."

Indeed, the dinner was no sooner finished than in rushed the Scarecrow, to hug Dorothy in his padded arms and tell her how glad he was to see her again. The Wizard was also most heartily welcomed by the straw man, who was an important personage in the Land of Oz.

"How are your brains?" inquired the little humbug, as he grasped the soft, stuffed hands of his old friend.

"Working finely," answered the Scarecrow. "I'm very certain, Oz, that you gave me the best brains in the world, for I can think with them day and night, when all other brains are fast asleep."

"How long did you rule the Emerald City, after I left here?" was the next question.

"Quite awhile, until I was conquered by a girl named General Jinjur. But Ozma soon conquered her, with the help of Glinda the Good, and after that I went to live with Nick Chopper, the Tin Woodman."

Just then a loud cackling was heard outside; and, when a servant threw open the door with a low bow, a yellow hen strutted in. Dorothy sprang forward and caught the fluffy fowl in her arms, uttering at the same time a glad cry.

"Oh, Billina!" she said. "How fat and sleek you've grown."

"Why shouldn't I?" asked the hen, in a sharp, clear voice. "I live on the fat of the land—don't I, Ozma?"

"You have everything you wish for," said the Princess.

Around Billina's neck was a string of beautiful pearls, and on her legs were bracelets of emeralds. She nestled herself comfortably in Dorothy's lap until the kitten gave a snarl of jealous anger and leaped up with a sharp claw fiercely bared to strike Billina a blow. But the little girl gave the angry kitten such a severe cuff that it jumped down again without daring to scratch.

"How horrid of you, Eureka!" cried Dorothy. "Is that the way to treat my friends?"

"You have queer friends, seems to me," replied the kitten in a surly tone.

"Seems to me the same way," said Billina scornfully, "if that beastly cat is one of them."

"Look here!" said Dorothy sternly. "I won't have any quarrelling in the Land of Oz, I can tell you! Everybody lives in peace here, and loves everybody else; and unless you two, Billina and Eureka, make up and be friends, I'll take my Magic Belt and wish you both home again, *immejitly*. So there!"

They were both much frightened at the threat, and promised meekly to be good. But it was never noticed that they became very warm friends, for all of that.

And now the Tin Woodman arrived, his body most beautifully nickel-plated, so that it shone splendidly in the brilliant light of the room. The Tin Woodman loved Dorothy most tenderly, and welcomed with joy the return of the little old Wizard.

"Sir," said he to the latter, "I never can thank you enough for the excellent heart you once gave me. It has made me many friends, I assure you, and it beats as kindly and lovingly today as it ever did."

"I'm glad to hear that," said the Wizard. "I was afraid it would get moldy in that tin body of yours."

"Not at all," returned Nick Chopper. "It keeps finely, being preserved in my airtight chest."

Zeb was a little shy when first introduced to these queer people; but they were so friendly and sincere that he soon grew to admire them very much, even finding some good qualities in the yellow hen. But he became nervous again when the next visitor was announced.

"This," said Princess Ozma, "is my friend Mr. H. M. Woggle-Bug, T. E., who assisted me one time when I was in great distress, and is now the Dean of the Royal College of Athletic Science."

"Ah," said the Wizard, "I'm pleased to meet so distinguished a personage."

"H. M.," said the Woggle-Bug pompously, "means Highly Magnified, and T. E. means Thoroughly Educated. I am, in reality, a very big bug, and doubtless the most intelligent being in all this broad domain."

"How well you disguise it," said the Wizard. "But I don't doubt your word in the least."

"Nobody doubts it, sir," replied the Woggle-Bug, and drawing a book from its pocket the strange insect turned its back on the company and sat down in a corner to read.

Nobody minded this rudeness, which might have seemed more impolite in one less thoroughly educated; so they straightaway forgot him and joined in a merry conversation that kept them well amused until bedtime arrived.

Chapter 16
Jim, the Cab-Horse

Jim the Cab-horse found himself in possession of a large room with a green marble floor and carved marble wainscoting, which was so stately in its appearance that it would have awed anyone else. Jim accepted it as a mere detail, and at his command the attendants gave his coat a good rubbing, combed his mane and tail, and washed his hoofs and fetlocks. Then they told him dinner would be served directly and he replied that they could not serve it too quickly to suit his convenience. First they brought him a steaming bowl of soup, which the horse eyed in dismay.

"Take that stuff away!" he commanded. "Do you take me for a salamander?"

They obeyed at once, and next served a fine large turbot on a silver platter, with drawn gravy poured over it.

"Fish!" cried Jim with a sniff. "Do you take me for a tomcat? Away with it!"

The servants were a little discouraged, but soon they brought in a great tray containing two dozen nicely roasted quail on toast.

"Well, well!" said the horse, now thoroughly provoked. "Do you take me for a weasel? How stupid and ignorant you are in the Land of Oz, and what dreadful things you feed upon! Is there nothing that is decent to eat in this palace?"

The trembling servants sent for the Royal Steward, who came in haste and said:

"What would your Highness like for dinner?"

"Highness!" repeated Jim, who was unused to such titles.

"You are at least six feet high, and that is higher than any other animal in this country," said the Steward.

"Well, my Highness would like some oats," declared the horse.

"Oats? We have no whole oats," the Steward replied, with much deference. "But there is any quantity of oatmeal, which we often cook for breakfast. Oatmeal is a breakfast dish," added the Steward humbly.

"I'll make it a dinner dish," said Jim. "Fetch it on, but don't cook it, as you value your life."

You see, the respect shown the worn-out old cab-horse made him a little arrogant, and he forgot he was a guest, never having been treated otherwise than as a servant since the day he was born, until his arrival in the Land of Oz. But the royal attendants did not heed the animal's ill temper. They soon mixed a tub of oatmeal with a little water, and Jim ate it with much relish.

Then the servants heaped a lot of rugs upon the floor and the old horse slept on the softest bed he had ever known in his life.

In the morning, as soon as it was daylight, he resolved to take a walk and try to find some grass for breakfast; so he ambled calmly through the handsome arch of the doorway, turned the corner of the palace, wherein all seemed asleep, and came face to face with the Sawhorse.

Jim stopped abruptly, being startled and amazed. The Sawhorse stopped at the same time and stared at the other with its queer protruding eyes, which were mere knots in the log that formed its body. The legs of the Sawhorse were four sticks driven into holes bored in the log; its tail was a small branch that had been left by accident and its mouth a place chopped in one end of the body which projected a little and served as a head. The ends of the wooden legs were shod with plates of solid gold, and the saddle of the Princess Ozma, which was of red leather set with sparkling diamonds, was strapped to the clumsy body.

Jim's eyes stuck out as much as those of the Sawhorse, and he stared at the creature with his ears erect and his long head drawn back until it rested against his arched neck.

In this comical position the two horses circled slowly around each other for a while, each being unable to realize what the singular thing might be which it now beheld for the first time. Then Jim exclaimed:

''For goodness sake, what sort of a being are you?''

"I'm a Sawhorse," replied the other.

"Oh; I believe I've heard of you," said the cab-horse. "But you are unlike anything that I expected to see."

"I do not doubt it," the Sawhorse observed, with a tone of pride. "I am considered quite unusual."

"You are, indeed. But a rickety wooden thing like you has no right to be alive."

"I couldn't help it," returned the other, rather crestfallen. "Ozma sprinkled me with a magic powder, and I just had to live. I know I'm not much account; but I'm the only horse in all the Land of Oz, so they treat me with great respect."

"You, a horse!"

"Oh, not a real one, of course. There are no real horses here at all. But I'm a splendid imitation of one."

Jim gave an indignant neigh.

"Look at me!" he cried. "Behold a real horse!"

The wooden animal gave a start, and then examined the other intently.

"Is it possible that you are a Real Horse?" he murmured.

"Not only possible, but true," replied Jim, who was gratified by the impression he had created. "It is proved by my fine points. For example, look at the long hairs on my tail, with which I can whisk away the flies."

"The flies never trouble me," said the Sawhorse.

"And notice my great strong teeth, with which I nibble the grass."

"It is not necessary for me to eat," observed the Sawhorse.

"Also examine my broad chest, which enables me to draw deep, full breaths," said Jim proudly.

"I have no need to breathe," returned the other.

"No; you miss many pleasures," remarked the cab-horse pityingly. "You do not know the relief of brushing away a fly that has bitten you, nor the delight of eating delicious food, nor the satisfaction of drawing a long breath of fresh, pure air. You may be an imitation of a horse, but you're a mighty poor one."

"Oh, I cannot hope ever to be like you," sighed the Sawhorse. "But I am glad to meet at last a Real Horse. You are certainly the most beautiful creature I ever beheld."

This praise won Jim completely. To be called beautiful was a novelty in his experience. Said he:

"Your chief fault, my friend, is in being made of wood, and that I suppose you cannot help. Real horses, like myself, are made of flesh and blood and bones."

"I can see the bones all right," replied the Sawhorse, "and they are admirable and distinct. Also I can see the flesh. But the blood, I suppose, is tucked away inside."

"Exactly," said Jim.

"What good is it?" asked the Sawhorse.

Jim did not know, but he would not tell the Sawhorse that.

"If anything cuts me," he replied, "the blood runs out to show where I am cut. You, poor thing, cannot even bleed when you are hurt."

"But I am never hurt," said the Sawhorse. "Once in a while I get broken up some, but I am easily repaired and put in good order again. And I never feel a break or a splinter in the least."

Jim was almost tempted to envy the wooden horse for being unable to feel pain; but the creature was so absurdly unnatural that he decided he would not change places with it under any circumstances.

"How did you happen to be shod with gold?" he asked.

"Princess Ozma did that," was the reply, "and it saves my legs from wearing out. We've had a good many adventures together, Ozma and I, and she likes me."

The cab-horse was about to reply when suddenly he gave a start and a neigh of terror and stood trembling like a leaf. For around the corner had come two enormous savage beasts, treading so lightly that they were upon him before he was aware of their presence. Jim was in the act of plunging down the path to escape when the Sawhorse cried out:

"Stop, my brother! Stop, Real Horse! These are friends, and will do you no harm."

Jim hesitated, eyeing the beasts fearfully. One was an enormous Lion with clear, intelligent eyes, a tawny mane bushy and well kept, and a body like yellow plush. The other was a great Tiger with purple stripes around his lithe body, powerful limbs, and eyes that showed through the half-closed lids like coals of fire. The huge forms of these monarchs of the forest and jungle were enough to strike terror to the stoutest heart, and it is no wonder Jim was afraid to face them.

But the Sawhorse introduced the stranger in a calm tone, saying:

"This, noble Horse, is my friend the Cowardly Lion, who is the valiant King of the Forest, but at the same time a faithful vassal of Princess Ozma. And this is the Hungry Tiger, the terror of the jungle, who longs to devour fat babies but is prevented by his conscience from doing so. These royal beasts are both warm friends of little Dorothy and have come to the Emerald City this morning to welcome her to our fairyland."

Hearing these words Jim resolved to conquer his alarm. He bowed his head with as much dignity as he could muster toward the savage-looking beasts, who in return nodded in a friendly way.

"Is not the Real Horse a beautiful animal?" asked the Sawhorse admiringly.

"That is doubtless a matter of taste," returned the Lion. "In the forest he would be thought ungainly, because his face is stretched out and his neck is uselessly long. His joints, I notice, are swollen and overgrown, and he lacks flesh and is old in years."

"And dreadfully tough," added the Hungry Tiger in a sad voice. "My conscience would never permit me to eat so tough a morsel as the Real Horse."

"I'm glad of that," said Jim; "for I, also, have a conscience, and it tells me not to crush in your skull with a blow of my powerful hoof."

If he thought to frighten the striped beast by such language he was mistaken. The Tiger seemed to smile, and winked one eye slowly.

"You have a good conscience, friend Horse," it said, "and if you attend to its teachings it will do much to protect you from harm. Some day I will let you try to crush in my skull, and afterward you will know more about tigers than you do now."

"Any friend of Dorothy," remarked the Cowardly Lion, "must be our friend, as well. So let us cease this talk of skull crushing and converse upon more pleasant subjects. Have you breakfasted, Sir Horse?"

"Not yet," replied Jim. "But here is plenty of excellent clover, so if you will excuse me I will eat now."

"He's a vegetarian," remarked the Tiger, as the horse began to munch the clover. "If I could eat grass I would not need a conscience, for nothing could then tempt me to devour babies and lambs."

Just then Dorothy, who had risen early and heard the voices of the animals, ran out to greet her old friends. She hugged both the Lion and the Tiger with eager delight, but seemed to love the King of Beasts a little better than she did his hungry friend, having known him longer.

By the time they had indulged in a good talk and Dorothy had told them all about the awful earthquake and her recent adventures, the breakfast bell rang from the palace and the little girl went inside to join her human comrades. As she entered the great hall a voice called out, in a rather harsh tone:

"What! Are *you* here again?"

"Yes, I am," she answered, looking all around to see where the voice came from.

"What brought you back?" was the next question, and Dorothy's eye rested on an antlered head hanging on the wall just over the fireplace, and caught its lips in the act of moving.

"Good gracious!" she exclaimed. "I thought you were stuffed."

"So I am," replied the head. "But once on a time I was part of the Gump, which Ozma sprinkled with the Powder of Life. I was then for a time the head of the finest Flying Machine that was ever known to exist, and we did many wonderful things. Afterward the Gump was taken apart and I was put back on this wall; but I can still talk when I feel in the mood, which is not often."

"It's very strange," said the girl. "What were you when you were first alive?"

"That I have forgotten," replied the Gump's Head, "and I do not think it is of much importance. But here comes Ozma; so I'd better hush up, for the Princess doesn't like me to chatter since she changed her name from Tip to Ozma."

Just then the girlish Ruler of Oz opened the door and greeted Dorothy with a good-morning kiss. The little Princess seemed fresh and rosy and in good spirits.

"Breakfast is served, dear," she said, "and I am hungry. So don't let us keep it waiting a single minute."

Chapter 17
The Nine Tiny Piglets

After breakfast Ozma announced that she had ordered a holiday to be observed throughout the Emerald City, in honor of her visitors. The people had learned that their old Wizard had returned to them and all were anxious to see him again, for he had always been a rare favorite. So first there was to be a grand procession through the streets, after which the little old man was requested to perform some of his wizardries in the great Throne Room of the palace. In the afternoon there were to be games and races.

The procession was very imposing. First came the Imperial Cornet Band of Oz, dressed in emerald velvet uniforms with slashes of pea-green satin and buttons of immense cut emeralds. They played the national air called "The Oz Spangled Banner," and behind them were the standard bearers with the royal flag.

This flag was divided into four quarters, one being colored sky blue, another pink, a third lavender and a fourth white. In the center was a large emerald-green star, and all over the four quarters were sewn spangles that glittered beautifully in the sunshine. The colors represented the four countries of Oz, and the green star the Emerald City.

Just behind the royal standard-bearers came the Princess Ozma in her royal chariot, which was of gold encrusted with emeralds and diamonds set in exquisite designs. The chariot was drawn on this occasion by the Cowardly Lion and the Hungry Tiger, who were decorated with immense pink and blue bows. In the chariot rode Ozma and Dorothy, the former in splendid raiment and wearing her royal coronet, while the little Kansas girl wore around her waist the Magic Belt she had once captured from the Nome King.

Following the chariot came the Scarecrow mounted on the Sawhorse, and the people cheered him almost as loudly as they did their lovely Ruler. Behind him stalked with regular, jerky steps, the famous machine man called Tik-tok, who had been wound up by Dorothy for the occasion. Tik-tok moved by clockwork, and was made all of burnished copper. He really belonged to the Kansas girl, who had much respect for his thoughts after they had been properly wound and set going; but as the copper man would be useless in any place but a fairy country Dorothy had left him in charge of Ozma, who saw that he was suitably cared for.

There followed another band after this, which was called the Royal Court Band, because the members all lived in the palace. They wore white uniforms with real diamond buttons and played "What is Oz without Ozma" very sweetly.

Then came Professor Woggle-Bug, with a group of students from the Royal College of Scientific Athletics. The boys wore long hair and striped sweaters and yelled their college yell every other step they took, to the great satisfaction of the populace, which was glad to have this evidence that their lungs were in good condition.

The brilliantly polished Tin Woodman marched next, at the head of the Royal Army of Oz which consisted of twenty-eight officers, from Generals down to Captains. There were no privates in the army because all were so courageous and skillful that they had been promoted one by one until there were no privates left. Jim and the buggy followed, the old cab-horse being driven by Zeb while the Wizard stood up on the seat and bowed his bald head right and left in answer to the cheers of the people, who crowded thick about him.

Taken altogether the procession was a grand success, and when it had returned to the palace the citizens crowded into the great Throne Room to see the Wizard perform his tricks.

The first thing the little humbug did was to produce a tiny white piglet from underneath his hat and pretend to pull it apart, making two. This act he repeated until all of the nine tiny piglets were visible, and they were so glad to get out of his pocket that they ran around in a very lively manner. The pretty little creatures would have been a novelty anywhere, so the people were as amazed and delighted at their appearance as even the Wizard could have desired. When he had made them all disappear again Ozma declared she was sorry they were gone, for she wanted one of them to pet and play with. So the Wizard pretended to take one of the piglets out of the hair of the Princess (while really he slyly took it from his inside pocket) and Ozma smiled joyously as the creature nestled in her arms, and she promised to have an emerald collar made for its fat neck and to keep the little squealer always at hand to amuse her.

Afterward it was noticed that the Wizard always performed his famous trick with eight piglets, but it seemed to please the people just as well as if there had been nine of them.

In his little room back of the Throne Room the Wizard had found a lot of things he had left behind him when he went away in the balloon, for no one had occupied the apartment in his absence. There was enough material there to enable him to prepare several new tricks which he had learned from some of the jugglers in the circus, and he had passed part of the night in getting them ready. So he followed the trick of the nine tiny piglets with several other wonderful feats that greatly delighted his audience and the people did not seem to care a bit whether the little man was a humbug Wizard or not, so long as he succeeded in amusing them. They applauded all his tricks and at the end of the performance begged him earnestly not to go away again and leave them.

"In that case," said the little man, gravely, "I will cancel all of my engagements before the crowned heads of Europe and America and devote myself to the people of Oz, for I love you all so well that I can deny you nothing."

After the people had been dismissed with this promise our friends joined Princess Ozma at an elaborate luncheon in the palace, where even the Tiger and the Lion were sumptuously fed and Jim the Cab-horse ate his oatmeal out of a golden bowl with seven rows of rubies, sapphires, and diamonds set around the rim of it.

In the afternoon they all went to a great field outside the city gates where the games were to be held. There was a beautiful canopy for Ozma and her guests to sit under and watch the people run races and jump and wrestle. You may be sure the folks of Oz did their best with such a distinguished company watching them, and finally Zeb offered to wrestle with a little Munchkin who seemed to be the champion. In appearance he was twice as old as Zeb, for he had long pointed whiskers and wore a peaked hat with little bells all around the brim of it, which tinkled gaily as he moved. But although the Munchkin was hardly tall enough to come to Zeb's shoulder he was so strong and clever that he laid the boy three times on his back with apparent ease.

Zeb was greatly astonished at his defeat, and when the pretty Princess joined her people in laughing at him he proposed a boxing match with the Munchkin, to which the little Ozite readily agreed. But the first time that Zeb managed to give him a sharp box on the ears the Munchkin sat down upon the ground and cried until the tears ran down his whiskers, because he had been hurt. This made Zeb laugh, in turn, and the boy felt comforted to find that Ozma laughed as merrily at her weeping subject as she had at him.

Just then the Scarecrow proposed a race between the Sawhorse and the Cab-horse; and although all the others were delighted at the suggestion the Sawhorse drew back, saying:

"Such a race would not be fair."

"Of course not," added Jim with a touch of scorn. "Those little wooden legs of yours are not half as long as my own."

"It isn't that," said the Sawhorse modestly. "But I never tire, and you do."

"Bah!" cried Jim, looking with great disdain at the other. "Do you imagine for an instant that such a shabby imitation of a horse as you are can run as fast as I?"

"I don't know, I'm sure," replied the Sawhorse.

"That is what we are trying to find out," remarked the Scarecrow. "The object of a race is to see who can win it—or at least that is what my excellent brains think."

"Once, when I was young," said Jim, "I was a race horse, and defeated all who dared run against me. I was born in Kentucky, you know, where all the best and most aristocratic horses come from.''

''But you're old now, Jim,'' suggested Zeb.

''Old! Why, I feel like a colt today,'' replied Jim. ''I only wish there was a real horse here for me to race with. I'd show the people a fine sight, I can tell you.''

''Then why not race with the Sawhorse?'' inquired the Scarecrow.

''He's afraid,'' said Jim.

''Oh, no,'' answered the Sawhorse. ''I merely said it wasn't fair. But if my friend the Real Horse is willing to undertake the race I am quite ready.''

So they unharnessed Jim and took the saddle off the Sawhorse, and the two queerly matched animals were stood side by side for the start.

''When I say 'Go!' '' Zeb called to them, ''you must dig out and race until you reach those three trees you see over yonder. Then circle 'round them and come back again. The first one that passes the place where the Princess sits shall be named the winner. Are you ready?''

''I suppose I ought to give the wooden dummy a good start of me,'' growled Jim.

''Never mind that,'' said the Sawhorse. ''I'll do the best I can.''

''Go!'' cried Zeb, and at the word the two horses leaped forward and the race was begun.

Jim's big hoofs pounded away at a great rate, and although he did not look very graceful he ran in a way to do credit to his Kentucky breeding. But the Sawhorse was swifter than the wind. Its wooden legs moved so fast that their twinkling could scarcely be seen, and although so much smaller than the cab-horse it covered the ground much faster. Before they had reached the trees the Sawhorse was far ahead, and the wooden animal returned to the starting place and was being lustily cheered by the Ozites before Jim came panting up to the canopy where the Princess and her friends were seated.

I am sorry to record the fact that Jim was not only ashamed of his defeat but for a moment lost control of his temper. As he looked at the comical face of the Sawhorse he imagined that the creature was laughing at him; so in a fit of unreasonable anger he turned around and made a vicious kick that sent his rival tumbling head over heels upon the ground, and broke off one of its legs and its left ear.

An instant later the Tiger crouched and launched its huge body through the air swift and resistless as a ball from a cannon. The beast struck Jim full on his shoulder and sent the astonished cab-horse rolling over and over, amid shouts of delight from the spectators, who had been horrified by the ungracious act he had been guilty of.

When Jim came to himself and sat upon his haunches he found the Cowardly Lion crouched on one side of him and the Hungry Tiger on the other, and their eyes were glowing like balls of fire.

"I beg your pardon, I'm sure," said Jim meekly. "I was wrong to kick the Sawhorse, and I am sorry I became angry at him. He has won the race, and won it fairly; but what can a horse of flesh do against a tireless beast of wood?"

Hearing this apology the Tiger and the Lion stopped lashing their tails and retreated with dignified steps to the side of the Princess.

"No one must injure one of our friends in our presence," growled the Lion; and Zeb ran to Jim and whispered that unless he controlled his temper in the future he would probably be torn to pieces.

Then the Tin Woodman cut a straight and strong limb from a tree with his gleaming axe and made a new leg and a new ear for the Sawhorse; and when they had been securely fastened in place Princess Ozma took the coronet from her own head and placed it upon that of the winner of the race. Said she:

"My friend, I reward you for your swiftness by proclaiming you Prince of Horses, whether of wood or of flesh; and hereafter all other horses—in the Land of Oz, at least—must be considered imitations, and you the real champion of your race."

There was more applause at this, and then Ozma had the jewelled saddle replaced upon the Sawhorse and herself rode the victor back to the city at the head of the grand procession.

"I ought to be a fairy," grumbled Jim as he slowly drew the buggy home; "for to be just an ordinary horse in a fairy country is to be of no account whatever. It's no place for us, Zeb."

"It's lucky we got here, though," said the boy; and Jim thought of the dark cave, and agreed with him.

Chapter 18

The Trial of Eureka the Kitten

Several days of festivity and merrymaking followed, for such old friends did not often meet and there was much to be told and talked over between them, and many amusements to be enjoyed in this delightful country.

Ozma was happy to have Dorothy beside her, for girls of her own age with whom it was proper for the Princess to associate were very few, and often the youthful Ruler of Oz was lonely for lack of companionship.

It was the third morning after Dorothy's arrival, and she was sitting with Ozma and their friends in a reception room, talking over old times, when the Princess said to her maid: "Please go to my boudoir, Jellia, and get the white piglet I left on the dressing table. I want to play with it."

Jellia at once departed on the errand, and she was gone so long that they had almost forgotten her mission when the green-robed maiden returned with a troubled face.

"The piglet is not there, your Highness," said she.

"Not there!" exclaimed Ozma. "Are you sure?"

"I have hunted in every part of the room," the maid replied.

"Was not the door closed?" asked the Princess.

"Yes, your Highness, I am sure it was. For when I opened it, Dorothy's white kitten crept out and ran up the stairs."

Hearing this, Dorothy and the Wizard exchanged startled glances, for they remembered how often Eureka had longed to eat a piglet. The little girl jumped up at once.

"Come, Ozma," she said anxiously; "let us go ourselves to search for the piglet."

So the two went to the dressing room of the Princess and searched carefully in every corner and among the vases and baskets and ornaments that stood about the pretty boudoir. But not a trace could they find of the tiny creature they sought.

Dorothy was nearly weeping by this time, while Ozma was angry and indignant. When they returned to the others the Princess said:

"There is little doubt that my pretty piglet has been eaten by that horrid kitten, and if that is true the offender must be punished."

"I don't b'lieve Eureka would do such a dreadful thing!" cried Dorothy, much distressed. "Go and get my kitten, please, Jellia, and we'll hear what she has to say about it."

The green maiden hastened away, but presently returned and said:

"The kitten will not come. She threatened to scratch my eyes out if I touched her."

"Where is she?" asked Dorothy.

"Under the bed in your own room," was the reply.

So Dorothy ran to her room and found the kitten under the bed.

"Come here, Eureka!" she said.

"I won't," answered the kitten in a surly voice.

"Oh, Eureka! Why are you so bad?"

The kitten did not reply.

"If you don't come to me right away," continued Dorothy, getting provoked, "I'll take my Magic Belt and wish you in the country of the Gurgles."

"Why do you want me?" asked Eureka, disturbed by this threat.

"You must go to Princess Ozma. She wants to talk to you."

"All right," returned the kitten, creeping out. "I'm not afraid of Ozma—or anyone else."

Dorothy carried her in her arms back to where the others sat in grieved and thoughtful silence.

"Tell me, Eureka," said the Princess gently: "Did you eat my pretty piglet?"

"I won't answer such a foolish question," asserted Eureka, with a snarl.

"Oh, yes you will, dear," Dorothy declared. "The piglet is gone, and you ran out of the room when Jellia opened the door. So, if you are innocent, Eureka, you must tell the Princess how you came to be in her room, and what has become of the piglet."

"Who accuses me?" asked the kitten defiantly.

"No one," answered Ozma. "Your actions alone accuse you. The fact is that I left my little pet in my dressing room lying asleep upon the table; and you must have stolen in without my knowing it. When next the door was opened you ran out and hid yourself—and the piglet was gone."

"That's none of my business," growled the kitten.

"Don't be impudent, Eureka," admonished Dorothy.

"It is you who are impudent," said Eureka, "for accusing me of such a crime when you can't prove it except by guessing."

Ozma was now greatly incensed by the kitten's conduct. She summoned her Captain-General, and when the long, lean officer appeared she said:

"Carry this cat away to prison, and keep her in safe confinement until she is tried by law for the crime of murder."

So the Captain-General took Eureka from the arms of the now weeping Dorothy and in spite of the kitten's snarls and scratches carried it away to prison.

"What shall we do now?" asked the Scarecrow with a sigh, for such a crime had cast a gloom over all the company.

"I will summon the Court to meet in the Throne Room at three o'clock," replied Ozma. "I myself will be the judge, and the kitten shall have a fair trial."

"What will happen if she is guilty?" asked Dorothy.

"She must die," answered the Princess.

"Nine times?" inquired the Scarecrow.

"As many times as is necessary," was the reply. "I will ask the Tin Woodman to defend the prisoner, because he has such a kind heart I am sure he will do his best to save her. And the Woggle-Bug shall be the Public Accuser, because he is so learned that no one can deceive him."

"Who will be the jury?" asked the Tin Woodman.

"There ought to be several animals on the jury," said Ozma, "because animals understand each other better than we people understand them. So the jury shall consist of the Cowardly Lion, the Hungry Tiger, Jim the Cab-horse, the Yellow Hen, the Scarecrow, the Wizard, Tik-tok the Machine Man, the Saw-horse, and Zeb of Hugson's Ranch. That makes the nine which the law requires, and all my people shall be admitted to hear the testimony."

They now separated to prepare for the sad ceremony; for whenever an appeal is made to law, sorrow is almost certain to follow—even in a fairyland like Oz. But it must be stated that the people of that Land were generally so well-behaved that there was not a single lawyer amongst them, and it had been years since any Ruler had sat in judgment upon an offender of the law. The crime of murder being the most dreadful crime of all, tremendous excitement prevailed in the Emerald City when the news of Eureka's arrest and trial became known.

The Wizard, when he returned to his own

room, was exceedingly thoughtful. He had no doubt Eureka had eaten his piglet, but he realized that a kitten cannot be depended upon at all times to act properly, since its nature is to destroy small animals and even birds for food, and the tame cat that we keep in our houses today is descended from the wild cat of the jungle—a very ferocious creature indeed. The Wizard knew that if Dorothy's pet was found guilty and condemned to death the little girl would be made very unhappy; so, although he grieved over the piglet's sad fate as much as any of them, he resolved to save Eureka's life.

Sending for the Tin Woodman, the Wizard took him into a corner and whispered:

"My friend, it is your duty to defend the white kitten and try to save her, but I fear you will fail because Eureka has long wished to eat a piglet, to my certain knowledge, and my opinion is that she has been unable to resist the temptation. Yet her disgrace and death would not bring back the piglet, but only serve to make Dorothy unhappy. So I intend to prove the kitten's innocence by a trick."

He drew from his inside pocket one of the eight tiny piglets that were remaining and continued:

"This creature you must hide in some safe place, and if the jury decides that Eureka is guilty you may then produce this piglet and claim it is the one that was lost. All the piglets are exactly alike, so no one can dispute your word. This deception will save Eureka's life, and then we may all be happy again."

"I do not like to deceive my friends," replied the Tin Woodman. "Still, my kind heart urges me to save Eureka's life, and I can usually trust my heart to do the right thing. So I will do as you say, friend Wizard."

After some thought he placed the little pig inside his funnel-shaped hat, and then put the hat upon his head and went back to his room to think over his speech to the jury.

Chapter 19

The Wizard Performs Another Trick

At three o'clock the Throne Room was crowded with citizens, men, women and children being eager to witness the great trial.

Princess Ozma, dressed in her most splendid robes of state, sat in the magnificent emerald throne, with her jewelled scepter in her hand and her sparkling coronet upon her fair brow. Behind her throne stood the twenty-eight officers of her army and many officials of the royal household. At her right sat the queerly assorted jury—animals, animated dummies, and people—all gravely prepared to listen to what was said. The kitten had been placed in a large cage just before the throne, where she sat upon her haunches and gazed through the bars at the crowds around her, with seeming unconcern.

And now, at a signal from Ozma, the Woggle-Bug arose and addressed the jury. His tone was pompous and he strutted up and down in an absurd attempt to appear dignified.

"Your Royal Highness and Fellow Citizens," he began; "the small cat you see a prisoner before you is accused of the crime of first murdering and then eating our esteemed ruler's fat piglet—or else first eating and then murdering it. In either case a grave crime has been committed which deserves a grave punishment."

"Do you mean my kitten must be put in a grave?" asked Dorothy.

"Don't interrupt, little girl," said the Woggle-Bug. "When I get my thoughts arranged in good order I do not like to have anything upset them or throw them into confusion."

"If your thoughts were any good they wouldn't become confused," remarked the Scarecrow earnestly. "My thoughts are always—"

"Is this a trial of thoughts, or of kittens?" demanded the Woggle-Bug.

"It's a trial of one kitten," replied the Scarecrow. "But your manner is a trial to us all."

"Let the Public Accuser continue," called Ozma from her throne, "and I pray you do not interrupt him."

"The criminal who now sits before the court licking her paws," resumed the Woggle-Bug. "has long desired to unlawfully eat the fat piglet, which was no bigger than a mouse. And finally she made a wicked plan to satisfy her depraved appetite for pork. I can see her, in my mind's eye—"

"What's that?" asked the Scarecrow.

"I say I can see her in my mind's eye—"

"The mind has no eye," declared the Scarecrow. "It's blind."

"Your Highness," cried the Woggle-Bug, appealing to Ozma, "have I a mind's eye, or haven't I?"

"If you have, it is invisible," said the Princess.

"Very true," returned the Woggle-Bug, bowing. "I say I see the criminal, in my mind's eye, creeping stealthily into the room of our Ozma and secreting herself, when no one was looking, until the Princess had gone away and the door was closed. Then the murderer was alone with her helpless victim, the fat piglet, and I see her pounce upon the innocent creature and eat it up—"

"Are you still seeing with your mind's eye?" inquired the Scarecrow.

"Of course; how else could I see it? And we know the thing is true, because since the time of that interview there is no piglet to be found anywhere."

"I suppose if the cat had been gone, instead of the piglet, your mind's eye would see the piglet eating the cat," suggested the Scarecrow.

"Very likely," acknowledged the Woggle-Bug. "And now, Fellow Citizens and Creatures of the Jury, I assert that so awful a crime deserves death, and in the case of the ferocious criminal before you—who is now washing her face—the death penalty should be inflicted nine times."

There was great applause when the speaker sat down. Then the Princess spoke in a stern voice:

"Prisoner, what have you to say for yourself? Are you guilty, or not guilty?"

"Why, that's for you to find out," replied Eureka. "If you can prove I'm guilty, I'll be willing to die nine times, but a mind's eye is no proof, because the Woggle-Bug has no mind to see with."

"Never mind, dear," said Dorothy.

Then the Tin Woodman arose and said:

"Respected Jury and dearly beloved Ozma, I pray you not to judge this feline prisoner unfeelingly. I do not think the innocent kitten can be guilty, and surely it is unkind to accuse a luncheon of being a murder. Eureka is the sweet pet of a lovely little girl whom we all admire, and gentleness and innocence are her chief virtues. Look at the kitten's intelligent eyes." (Here Eureka closed her eyes sleepily.) "Gaze at her smiling countenance!" (Here Eureka snarled and showed her teeth.) "Mark the tender pose of her soft, padded little hands!" (Here Eureka bared her sharp claws and scratched at the bars of the cage.) "Would such a gentle animal be guilty of eating a fellow creature? No; a thousand times, no!"

"Oh, cut it short," said Eureka; "you've talked long enough."

"I'm trying to defend you," remonstrated the Tin Woodman.

"Then say something sensible," retorted the kitten. "Tell them it would be foolish for me to eat the piglet, because I had sense enough to know it would raise a row if I did. But don't try to make out I'm too innocent to eat a fat piglet if I could do it and not be found out. I imagine it would taste mighty good."

"Perhaps it would, to those who eat," remarked the Tin Woodman. "I myself, not being built to eat, have no personal experience in such matters. But I remember that our great poet once said:

> *'To eat is sweet*
> *When hunger's seat*
> *Demands a treat*
> *Of savory meat.'*

"Take this into consideration, friends of the Jury, and you will readily decide that the kitten is wrongfully accused and should be set at liberty."

When the Tin Woodman sat down no one applauded him, for his arguments had not been very convincing and few believed that he had proved Eureka's innocence. As for the Jury, the members whispered to each other for a few minutes and then they appointed the Hungry Tiger their spokesman. The huge beast slowly arose and said:

"Kittens have no consciences, so they eat whatever pleases them. The jury believes the white kitten known as Eureka is guilty of having eaten the piglet owned by Princess Ozma, and recommends that she be put to death in punishment of the crime."

The judgement of the jury was received with great applause, although Dorothy was sobbing miserably at the fate of her pet. The Princess was just about to order Eureka's head chopped off with the Tin Woodman's axe when that brilliant personage once more arose and addressed her.

"Your Highness," said he, "see how easy it is for a jury to be mistaken. The kitten could not have eaten your piglet—for here it is!"

He took off his funnel hat and from beneath it produced a tiny white piglet, which he held aloft that all might see it clearly.

Ozma was delighted and exclaimed eagerly:

"Give me my pet, Nick Chopper!"

And all the people cheered and clapped their hands, rejoicing that the prisoner had escaped death and been proved to be innocent.

As the Princess held the white piglet in her arms and stroked its soft hair, she said: "Let Eureka out of the cage, for she is no longer a prisoner, but our good friend. Where did you find my missing pet, Nick Chopper?"

"In a room of the palace," he answered.

"Justice," remarked the Scarecrow with a sigh, "is a dangerous thing to meddle with. If you hadn't happened to find the piglet, Eureka would surely have been executed."

"But justice prevailed at the last," said Ozma, "for here is my pet, and Eureka is once more free."

"I refuse to be free," cried the kitten in a sharp voice, "unless the Wizard can do his trick with eight piglets. If he can produce but seven, then this is not the piglet that was lost, but another one."

"Hush, Eureka!" warned the Wizard.

"Don't be foolish," advised the Tin Woodman, "or you may be sorry for it."

"The piglet that belonged to the Princess wore an emerald collar," said Eureka, loudly enough for all to hear.

"So it did!" exclaimed Ozma. "This cannot be the one the Wizard gave me."

"Of course not; he had nine of them, altogether," declared Eureka. "And I must say it was very stingy of him not to let me eat just a few. But now that this foolish trial is ended, I will tell you what really became of your pet piglet."

At this everyone in the Throne Room suddenly became quiet, and the kitten continued, in a calm, mocking tone of voice:

"I will confess that I intended to eat the little pig for my breakfast; so I crept into the room where it was kept while the Princess was dressing and hid myself under a chair. When Ozma went away she closed the door and left her pet on the table. At once I jumped up and told the piglet not to make a fuss, for he would be inside of me in half a second; but no one can teach one of these creatures to be reasonable. Instead of keeping still, so I could eat him comfortably, he trembled so with fear that he fell off the table into a big vase that was standing on the floor. The vase had a very small neck, and spread out at the top like a bowl. At first the piglet stuck in the neck of the vase and I thought I should get him after all, but he wriggled himself through and fell down into the deep bottom part—and I suppose he's there yet."

All were astonished at this confession, and Ozma at once sent an officer to her room to fetch the vase. When he returned, the Princess looked down the narrow neck of the big ornament and discovered her lost piglet, just as Eureka had said she would.

There was no way to get the creature out without breaking the vase, so the Tin Woodman smashed it with his axe and set the little prisoner free.

Then the crowd cheered lustily and Dorothy hugged the kitten in her arms and told her how delighted she was to know that she was innocent.

"But why didn't you tell us at first?" she asked.

"It would have spoiled the fun," replied the kitten, yawning.

Ozma gave the Wizard back the piglet he had so kindly allowed Nick Chopper to substitute for the lost one, and then she carried her own into the apartments of the palace where she lived. And now, the trial being over, the good citizens of the Emerald City scattered to their homes, well content with the day's amusement.

Chapter 20
Zeb Returns to the Ranch

Eureka was much surprised to find herself in disgrace; but she was, in spite of the fact that she had not eaten the piglet. For the folks of Oz knew the kitten had tried to commit the crime, and that only an accident had prevented her from doing so; therefore even the Hungry Tiger preferred not to associate with her. Eureka was forbidden to wander around the palace and was made to stay in confinement in Dorothy's room; so she began to beg her mistress to send her to some other place where she could enjoy herself better.

Dorothy was herself anxious to get home, so she promised Eureka they would not stay in the Land of Oz much longer.

The next evening after the trial the little girl begged Ozma to allow her to look in the enchanted picture, and the Princess readily consented. She took the child to her room and said: "Make your wish, dear, and the picture will show the scene you desire to behold."

Then Dorothy found, with the aid of the enchanted picture, that Uncle Henry had returned to the farm in Kansas, and she also saw that both he and Aunt Em were dressed in mourning, because they thought their little niece had been killed by the earthquake.

"Really," said the girl anxiously, "I must get back as soon as poss'ble to my own folks."

Zeb also wanted to see his home, and although he did not find anyone mourning for him, the sight of Hugson's Ranch in the picture made him long to get back there.

"This is a fine country, and I like all the people that live in it," he told Dorothy. "But the fact is, Jim and I don't seem to fit into a fairyland, and the old horse has been begging me to go home again ever since he lost the race. So, if you can find a way to fix it, we'll be much obliged to you."

"Ozma can do it, easily," replied Dorothy. "Tomorrow morning I'll go to Kansas and you can go to Californy."

That last evening was so delightful that the boy will never forget it as long as he lives. They were all together (except Eureka) in the pretty rooms of the Princess, and the Wizard did some new tricks, and the Scarecrow told stories, and the Tin Woodman sang a love song in a sonorous, metallic voice, and everybody laughed and had a good time. Then Dorothy wound up Tik-tok and he danced a jig to amuse the company, after which the Yellow Hen related some of her adventures with the Nome King in the Land of Ev.

The Princess served delicious refreshments to those who were in the habit of eating, and when Dorothy's bedtime arrived the company separated after exchanging many friendly sentiments.

Next morning they all assembled for the final parting, and many of the officials and courtiers came to look upon the impressive ceremonies.

Dorothy held Eureka in her arms and bade her friends a fond good-bye.

"You must come again some time," said the little Wizard; and she promised she would if she found it possible to do so.

"But Uncle Henry and Aunt Em need me to help them," she added, "so I can't ever be very long away from the farm in Kansas."

Ozma wore the Magic Belt; and, when she had kissed Dorothy farewell and had made her wish, the little girl and her kitten disappeared in a twinkling.

"Where is she?" asked Zeb, rather bewildered by the suddenness of it.

"Greeting her uncle and aunt in Kansas by this time," returned Ozma with a smile.

Then Zeb brought out Jim, all harnessed to the buggy, and took his seat.

"I'm much obliged for all your kindness," said the boy, "and very grateful to you for saving my life and sending me home again after all the good times I've had. I think this is the loveliest country in the world; but not being fairies Jim and I feel we ought to be where we belong—and that's at the ranch. Good-bye, everybody!"

He gave a start and rubbed his eyes. Jim was trotting along the well-known road, shaking his ears and whisking his tail with a contented motion. Just ahead of them were the gates of Hugson's Ranch, and Uncle Hugson now came out and stood with uplifted arms and wide-open mouth, staring in amazement.

"Good gracious! It's Zeb—and Jim, too!" he exclaimed. "Where in the world have you been, my lad?"

"Why, in the world, Uncle," answered Zeb with a laugh.